FLIGHT OF THE GARGOYLES

GARGOYLE GUARDIAN CHRONICLES BOOK 4

REBECCA CHASTAIN

M
Y
M

Copyright © 2022 by Rebecca Chastain
Excerpt from *Deadlines & Dryads* copyright © by Rebecca Chastain
Cover design by JoY Author Design Studio
Author photograph by Cody Watson

www.rebeccachastain.com

Mind Your Muse Books
PO Box 374
Rocklin, CA 95677

ISBN: 978-1-7344939-7-9

ALSO BY REBECCA CHASTAIN

Join Rebecca's VIP newsletter at RebeccaChastain.com!

For tossing out an idea that made me smile (and got me writing),
this one's for you, Mom.

Constructive Elements

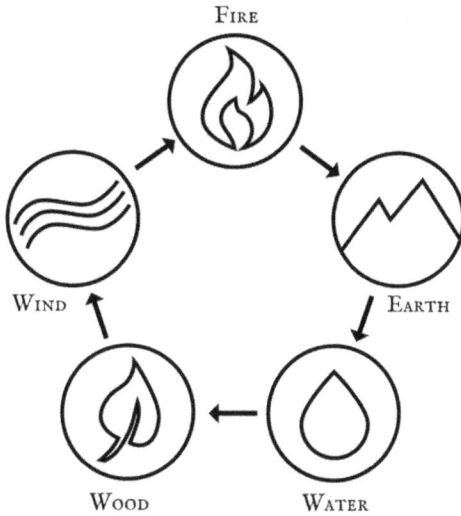

Fire

Wind

Earth

Wood

Water

Destructive Elements

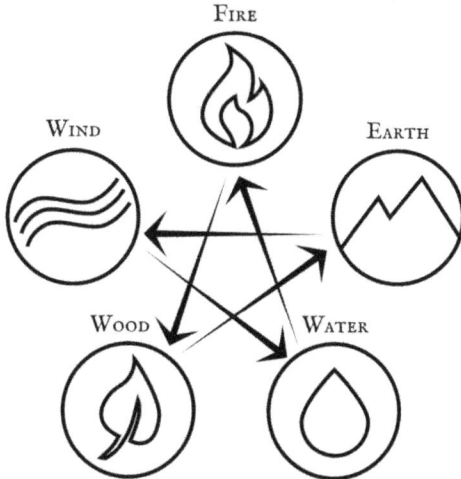

Fire

Wind

Earth

Wood

Water

1

"That's our ride?" I squeaked.

I checked Marcus's expression, hoping I had misheard him. His smile did nothing to ease the queasiness swelling in my stomach.

The shriek of tree branches clawing against wood made me jump. I spun to face my nightmare. A flimsy dirigible caromed between the cottonwoods lining the street, scraping its bottom against the upper canopies. Broken branches clattered to the cobblestones, splintering against the hard stone, and shredded leaves swirled into the air as the pilot pivoted the airborne abomination to thread the gap and descend toward the street. I cringed as nearby house wards snapped into place, anticipating my landlady's irritation even as I wished I could duck out of sight behind a ward of my own.

"It couldn't be more perfect," Marcus said. "It's quick, it's free—Patrick owes me—and best of all, it's going our way." He cupped an arm around my shoulders and pulled me against his warm side. "I didn't think we could reach the everlasting tree in time, Mika, but with this, we have a chance."

I tucked my head against his shoulder to hide my horrified expression. I wanted to see the everlasting tree, but . . . flying? Why did it have to be *flying*?

Up until a few days ago, finding the cure for local comatose gargoyles had consumed my focus. The everlasting tree's impending once-a-generation blooming hadn't been important—at least not once I determined I couldn't rely on it as a means for curing the gargoyles. Although the magical tree granted answers to seemingly impossible questions when it bloomed, no one knew exactly when the tree would release its knowledge. I hadn't been willing to leave the lives of the fading gargoyles to chance.

Now, with the comatose gargoyles on the mend and the tree yet to bloom, I had still resigned myself to missing the momentous experience. The everlasting tree was too far away. No trains stopped anywhere close to its grove, and even if we rented the city's fastest horses or powered up an air cart right now, it would take well over a week to reach the tree. Besides, we had only just returned to Terra Haven. My bags were still packed, my clothes still wrinkled from being slept in the night before. I had already decided to wash away the disappointment of missing the everlasting tree with a long soak in my bathtub.

I never considered flying. It was expensive and extravagant, and most important, terrifying. But Marcus Velasquez, a Federal Pentagon Defense warrior who never met a challenge he didn't tackle head on, wasn't scared of something as trivial as being suspended thousands of feet in the air on little more than a few planks of weathered wood, poised to fall to his death.

I glanced past Marcus's shoulder to Ms. Zuberrie's

stately Victorian, where I rented a room. Home. It was so close. My travel-frayed nerves needed a dose of the serenity that could be achieved only by being surrounded by my belongings. And my gargoyles.

I had sensed them from several blocks away, each a glowing bundle of energy inside my head, but nothing compared to seeing them in person. The four gargoyles talking animatedly on the eaves of the Victorian were as different as any collection of gargoyles—Lydia, a plump pink, purple, and orange agate swan with lion's feet; Anya, a sleek dumortierite-and-aventurine panther with wings that stretched nearly as long as her tail; Herbert, a compact dumortierite-veined rose-quartz armadillo with a toucan's beak and stubby wings; and Oliver, a slender carnelian dragon with eagle wings. Anyone unfamiliar with the quartet would never suspect they were siblings from the same clutch. Only Quinn was missing, having accompanied my best friend, Kylie, to the everlasting tree days earlier.

I barely had time for more than a cursory check of each gargoyle, assuring myself their living-quartz bodies radiated robust health, before Marcus whisked me back to the street. Oliver remained behind to share our recent adventures, but when he caught my gaze, whatever he saw in my expression made his wings unfurl in alarm. With a flick of his tail, he launched from the roof. His carnelian wings fractured the sunlight, bathing Marcus's face in an ominous crimson and flaring bloodred outlines around our shadows.

"What is it?" he asked, landing with a clatter of quartz paws.

I reached for Oliver, taking comfort in the smooth curves of his stone mane beneath my fingers.

"Nothing," I said. At least nothing that would make sense to him.

"Ahoy!" a male voice called from above.

Marcus released me to wave back. Thick coils of air and earth magic wove from his fingers and hooked the sinking dirigible, anchoring it to the street as it landed. Marcus wielded the bands of elements effortlessly, but it would have been just as easy to imagine him stopping the airship with sheer physical strength. Even in civilian clothes, Marcus looked the part of a warrior. It was partially his military-short black hair and partially his anvil jaw, but mainly it was the breadth of his shoulders and the muscles cording his body beneath his white cotton shirt and khaki trousers. Happiness glinted in his blue eyes as he strode toward the ship with his usual energetic grace, exhibiting none of the travel fatigue that clung to me.

If the dirigible hadn't loomed behind him, I might have possessed room in my brain to be self-conscious. Marcus was a powerful full-spectrum fire elemental who tenaciously defended Terra Haven from deadly monsters—human and otherwise. I, on the other hand, was a mid-level earth elemental with a quartz specialty. I could heal gargoyles, but until recently, I spent the majority of my time holed up in my room, fussing over commissioned quartz projects. On a good day, I appeared ordinary and insignificant. With my snarled braid, rumpled clothes, and teetering equilibrium, today wasn't a good day.

"Come on, Mika," Marcus called, waving me forward.

I fluttered a hand in his direction, my smile a grimace. *Let's go,* I urged my feet. *Before Marcus realizes I'm a complete coward.*

My boots remained fused to the cobblestones, my feet transformed into granite blocks.

Movement atop the ship gave me an excuse to jerk my gaze from Marcus's puzzled frown. A lanky black man strode across the airship's deck with the loose-kneed gait of a lifelong flier. Canary-yellow pants bagged around his thighs and cinched his calves just above lace-up leather boots. A form-fitting lime-and-yellow-striped shirt clung to his lean torso. What the outfit lacked in aesthetics it made up for in visibility, which was likely the point. With no regard for the neck-breaking drop to the cobblestones, the man leaned over the nominal railing and grinned down at Marcus.

"You're lucky you caught me before I left town, Velasquez. Another ten minutes, and I would have been gone."

"You would have turned back for me," Marcus said.

The pilot scoffed. "You? No. Her?" His gaze landed on me, and a slow smile pulled up the corner of his mouth. "You know how I feel about redheads. Those flaming locks are a siren song for my eyes."

Marcus grimaced at the mention of a siren. "Patrick, meet my girlfriend, Mika. Mika, this is my childhood friend, Patrick."

My stomach flipped. This was the first time Marcus had introduced me as his girlfriend, and I liked the way it sounded. Clumsily, I got my feet unstuck and shuffled toward the dirigible. Marcus retreated to meet me halfway, his eyes searching mine. I gave him a tremulous smile.

Patrick whistled. "Girlfriend, huh? You don't look big enough to have wrestled Velasquez into submission. You must have hidden talents or some really impressive"—his eyebrows waggled—"magic."

"Did I mention he's got the wit of a sixteen-year-old?" Marcus asked, shooting his friend a glare.

I forced a noncommittal noise past my numb lips. This close, it was impossible to ignore the airship or its striking resemblance to a diseased fish. Convoluted rigging secured faded chartreuse cloth sails against the bloated cabin like crumpled gills, and spells netted the entire ship in a distressing mesh of air and fire elements. Beneath the magic, more than one scrape cut through the flaking yellow paint, exposing raw wood. Six fragile ropes attached the slipshod craft to a slender cigar-shaped balloon, its canvas a sun-bleached exaggeration of Patrick's eye-popping green-and-yellow-striped top.

"Patrick, this is Oliver," Marcus continued. "He and Mika are a team. Oliver, you can ignore everything Patrick says. He's just a means to an end."

"Ouch." Patrick pretended to clutch his heart, but his eyes lit upon Oliver with open curiosity. "I would never disparage a gargoyle, especially not one as handsome as you, Oliver. Now, what are we waiting for? Come aboard, and we'll be off."

My stomach burrowed toward my toes, a ricochet of bile climbing my throat. Patrick flipped a rope ladder over the railing. Eyes unfocused, I watched dust motes explode from the twisted hemp when it smacked the side of the dirigible, and I carefully did not move. If I so much as twitched, I was afraid I would run and not stop until I locked and warded myself in my apartment.

Marcus tossed his bag to the deck, then my satchel, followed by my bag of seed crystals.

"Oyá's grace! What do you have in here? Rocks?" Patrick asked, staggering when he slung the strap over his shoulder.

"Close enough," Marcus said. He gestured me toward the ladder. "Come on. I'll steady it for you."

"Is it just me, or does this ship look like a death trap?" I asked, attempting to sound nonchalant but hoping Marcus would take a second look at the flimsy construction of the dirigible and agree.

He frowned. "You know there's nothing dangerous about it, right?"

"About this ship in particular or any airship?" Surely he understood that bobbing along in a wooden box supported by a hodgepodge of brash spell work, hot air, and fraying ropes was the definition of *dangerous*.

My calves knocked into Oliver, and I teetered, off balance. The gargoyle flared his wings in confusion. His bright eyes darted from my face to Marcus's, then back to me.

"I don't see anything bad. What am I missing?" Oliver reared onto his hind legs, spreading his stone wings wide. Unwittingly, he boxed me in, and I fought a flash of panic that insisted I push past him and flee to open ground.

If only I could escape my fear that easily.

"Nothing." Marcus rested a reassuring hand on Oliver's wing. "Mika, have you ever been on an airship?"

I bit my lip and shook my head. Air travel had never been in my budget. Besides, my fear of heights had always far outweighed any reason for launching myself into the atmosphere.

Until now.

Oliver settled on all four feet, folding his wings. With a soft whine, he twined his tail around my leg in silent support.

"Did you just refer to *Grasshopper's Grave* as a death trap?" Patrick asked, leaning over the edge as if he were going to dive headfirst to the cobblestones.

Marcus dropped his face into his palm.

"*Grave* is in its name?" I asked, my voice an octave too high.

"Patrick, you're not helping," Marcus growled.

Patrick tipped farther over the edge, one deep exhale away from toppling. His serious expression caught mine, the haunted depths of his tawny eyes aging him far beyond his twenty-something years. "It was two years ago on this very day. My first mate, a slight woman, not unlike yourself, Mika. She was so nimble on the ship, we called her a grasshopper. She could make any jump from any wing or rigging. Until one day . . . well, one day, she didn't." He scuffed his feet in a mock jump, then windmilled his arms to catch his balance.

I screamed, short and sharp, grabbing for the elements. Oliver's boost sang through me, and I whipped every ounce of air I could hold toward Patrick to shove him upright. My magic barely touched him, and he rocked back on his heels, having never needed my assistance. His head fell back, and his booming laugh echoed down the street.

Incredulous, I spun on Marcus. "That wasn't— I'm not— I can't—" I sputtered.

"Seriously?" Marcus asked, his head tipped back to glare at Patrick. "What's wrong with you?"

The pilot raised his hands. "Hey, she started it with that *death trap* insult."

Marcus shoved a hand through his thick hair, fisting a clump, but when he focused on me, his expression softened. "He's got a terrible sense of humor—"

"You think?"

"But he's a good pilot." Marcus took my hands, shaking them gently until I unclenched my jaw. His gaze searched mine, earnestness radiated from his blue eyes. "I wouldn't have set up this flight if it wasn't safe."

"I know," I said, not sounding the least bit convincing. But it was true. I trusted Marcus with my life. Not only that,

I loved him. With Marcus, I would always be safe—even on a perilous flying contraption like this.

My head knew it, my heart knew it, but my insides still quaked.

"It's a Message in a Bottle dirigible," Marcus said. "It's fast, safe, and reliable. The company wouldn't have it any other way."

I nodded. He wasn't saying anything I didn't know. Message in a Bottle had a long-standing reputation of excellence. I had used the company's services a few times around the holidays, and every spell-recorded message I sent had reached my parents and sister. I had never heard of one of their ships crashing.

"We also pride ourselves on being on time," Patrick interjected from above, "so if we could get go—"

Marcus's nostrils flared, and cold fire ignited in his eyes. When he glanced upward, Patrick's teeth clicked together.

Was I really going to do this? Was I going to spend multiple days dangling in the sky aboard an *airship*?

I crouched, embracing the need to get closer to the ground. Oliver dipped his head to peer at me. Sun soaked into the deep-red hues of his quartz scales, warming him beneath my hand. Breathing deep, I centered myself in his clean scent and comforting presence.

Marcus squatted in front of me, his wide frame blocking the bottom of the hovering dirigible from sight.

"Any other mode of transportation will be too slow," he said softly.

"I know."

"You can't make decisions based on fear. You have to follow what's in here." He tapped my breastbone over my heart.

Shame washed through me. I was supposed to be a

guardian of gargoyles. Protecting gargoyles was my duty, and if I worded my question for the everlasting tree cleverly, its answer could help countless gargoyles. I should have been like Marcus, doing everything in my power to get to the tree before it bloomed.

Yet here I hunched, knees quaking, scrambling for a reason to stay behind.

Marcus dropped his hand to my knee, and I blinked his face into focus. Why couldn't I be fearless like him?

It's an airship. People fly in them every day. I can do this.

And if I couldn't, what would Marcus think? The possibility of disappointing him made me ill. And Oliver . . . My friend stared at me with love and trust radiating from his dragon eyes. He expected me to behave like a gargoyle guardian. I couldn't let him down.

"Is *Grasshopper's Grave* really the ship's name?" I asked, stalling.

"No. It's *Breezy Bunny* or something like that."

"*Happy Hopper*," Patrick yelled over the side.

"And the woman who . . ." I dove a hand toward the ground to imitate her horrid death.

"Never existed," Marcus said.

I nodded. My head bobbed too many times, but Marcus didn't comment. I let out a shaky breath and forced myself to my feet.

"All right. Let's go."

2

Air rasped into my lungs, then out, fast and shallow. And noisy. It grated against my ears in the confined space, but it wasn't loud enough to drown out the dirigible's distressing groans and pops. A shudder wracked the *Happy Hopper*, rattling the narrow bunk where I huddled belowdecks. I clutched my knees to my chest and braced for a crash. The ship bobbed and recovered. My stomach flipped. Sweat plastered my shirt to my spine and stuck strands of hair to my face.

Oliver squeezed his body around me, crooning softly. I closed my eyes and tried to pretend we were somewhere safe. Like home, sitting on my bed. Only my bed was softer than this wooden slab. And stationary.

The airship lurched sideways, and a whimper escaped my throat. Glass and bronze bottles clinked a warning chorus as the ship's inventory shifted around me. I thought being down here, inside the ship rather than perched atop the precarious deck, would be easier. Here, I couldn't see how fast or high we sailed. In theory, it should have eased my anxiety.

Instead, it gave my imagination free rein.

A heavy bang reverberated from the left. I jumped, spinning toward the sound, expecting to see a hole punched through the ship's fragile frame. Were we under attack? Had we hit something? The ship bobbed, and my stomach lifted with the nose of the dirigible. Were we hurtling high into the clouds? Or were we falling backward? Dizziness made it impossible to tell.

Marcus's and Patrick's voices floated down the narrow staircase. I strained to catch their words. *Sinking.* Marcus clearly said something about us sinking. My body flushed hot, then cold. Or had he said "thinking"? He didn't sound scared, but then again, Marcus never did. In a crisis, he got calmer.

Marcus won't let Patrick wreck the ship. I'm safe, I told myself, but fear shredded my logic. How was I supposed to survive *days* like this? More important, how could I be a guardian to any gargoyle if I died on this airship?

I rocked in place, hot tears leaking from between my clenched eyelashes. I hated being this scared of something so irrational. But no amount of self-talk convinced my pulse to steady itself, not when every bump felt like the precursor of a crash.

Why had I gotten on this cursed dirigible?

Oxygen wheezed down my esophagus, my breaths rasping painfully. The ship capsized. My eyes flew open. The world straightened, then spun the other way. Saliva pooled in the back of my throat.

"I think I'm going—" I clamped a hand over my mouth as nausea rolled up my spine, and I fought it down. Sweat slithered down my cheek to drop from my chin, and I gasped in a beleaguered breath.

"It's too hot," I told Oliver. "I need air."

I lurched to my feet, then crashed to my knees when the ship tilted beneath me. My teeth smashed together painfully. Oliver whined, but I couldn't soothe him. Half crawling, half scrambling, I careened toward the stairs and the open hatch leading to the deck.

A shadow darkened the opening. "Mika?"

Feverish heat surged from my midsection to my forehead, tunneling my vision. I stubbed a toe against the bottom stair and flailed for the railing. Bands of air caught me, steadying me. Tipping my head, I met Marcus's concerned gaze. I had a second to experience the bone-deep dread of impending embarrassment, then my stomach's contents surged up my throat.

"Whoa. Easy, Mika. It's all right." My feet went airborne, and Marcus's arms were around me, holding me through the next bout of nausea. A pocket of solidified air captured the horrid projectile, sealing it inside.

Oh, lovely. My new boyfriend just caught my vomit.

Marcus spun fire around the disgusting liquid, incinerating it. Then he tossed the ash overboard.

I froze. The gray particulates puffed into nothingness against a cerulean sky. I was on the deck. High above the ground. How high, I couldn't tell, but I couldn't see the foothills or anything in the distance. Which meant we had to be very, very high.

Black spots danced in my vision. I swayed, and Marcus helped me to my knees. I sat back on my heels, then slid off them to sit sideways, one hand planted on the deck, wishing I could sink my nails into the lacquered surface for better purchase.

"Here, take a sip of this." Marcus handed me a canteen.

I accepted it blindly, rinsing the vile taste from my mouth. Oliver trundled up the stairs in awkward caterpillar-like scrunching hops until his wings cleared the hatch. Then he half flapped, half leapt to my side.

"What happened? Are you ill?" He snuffled my cheek and ran his cool muzzle down my arm.

I lifted a hand from the deck and latched on to Oliver. Holding his quartz body felt safer. He opened his boost to me, and I drew on the elements, attempting to steady my mind in the familiarity of our connection.

"Looks like your girl has a classic case of airsickness," Patrick said, his tone annoyingly carefree. Deck boards creaked as he approached, his shadow falling across us. "A bit of elevation evacuation. Some soar and spew."

I glowered at his boots. Friend of Marcus's or not, I was beginning to loathe Patrick.

"We get it," Marcus growled.

"Don't worry, Mika, most people only experience the ol' rise and retch their first few flights. You'll get your air legs soon. Faster than most, given our flight plan. Though . . ." Patrick tapped his chin thoughtfully. "The phrase doesn't technically work since we're going down. The ol' descend and disgorge? Eh, it's not as catchy."

Marcus growled something unintelligible under his breath.

"We're going down?" I asked, my brain latching on to the important words in Patrick's ramblings and setting them on repeat inside my skull.

"We'll land and be back in the air in no time," Marcus said. He smiled when he spoke.

I stared at him blankly. I had been belowdecks. I had seen the messages in their bottles. The *Happy Hopper* was a working delivery ship. Patrick had even talked about keeping to his schedule. I had all the facts, but I had failed to piece them together to realize we would need to descend and ascend *multiple times* before our final destination. I had envisioned us sailing straight to the everlasting tree.

The nose of the *Hopper* tipped earthward. The horizon came into view, shockingly close. I stopped breathing, blood draining from my head. Flying was dangerous, but at least the air was devoid of obstacles, save one. Below us, the entire planet was one giant crashing hazard.

"I'm going to give Patrick a hand," Marcus said. "Oliver, why don't you . . . ?" He stood and guided Oliver into his place. Oliver unfolded a wing across my legs, securing me to the deck. "Better?" Marcus asked.

I nodded. A thick tear rolled down my cheek, and Marcus gently brushed it aside. Another followed, my fear leaking out despite how hard I tried to suppress it. A subtle heat spell kissed my skin, pulling the sweat from my clothes and hair. I curled miserably around Oliver's wing, wishing I could disappear. If this airship didn't kill me, mortification would.

"Hang in there. You'll feel better soon." Marcus paused to gently cup my shoulders. "I won't let anything happen to you. You're safe, Mika."

The balloon vented air in a piercing whistle as he strode away. I jerked, knocking my knees against Oliver's sturdy wing. Gravity slackened, and wind tugged loose strands of my hair *upward*.

I scrambled for the elements, but adrenaline overload made me clumsy, and I couldn't get a solid grip on magic. Breaths hiccuping, I spun to call out to Marcus. If we were crashing, he would need my magic in the link. I had to get a hold—

Marcus waved at me from the rear of the ship, where he lounged against the railing with Patrick. Magic spun from both men, manipulating the balloon and flowing into spells hidden beneath the ship's belly. My runaway panic stuttered but refused to dissipate.

"You're safe, Mika," Oliver soothed. "I've got you."

Squeezing my eyes shut, I hunched over Oliver, and he hugged his wing tighter around me in return. I trusted him. I wanted to believe him, but I couldn't dismiss the voice in the back of my mind screaming that I was about to die—and so were the people I loved.

And I was helpless to do anything to stop it.

A sob escaped my throat, setting off a cascade of hot tears. Oliver rested his head on my shoulder and crooned a melody that teased at the edges of my memory. I tried to listen, but the ship kept rocking and sliding beneath me, and it was all I could do to not scream.

"Breathe, Mika," Oliver said, mid-croon. "With me. In . . . Out."

I gasped in breaths and sobbed them out three times faster than Oliver's inhalation. A warm hand settled on my back, and I whimpered, embarrassment flaring inside my fear. I tried to pull myself together, but I couldn't find an edge to grab hold of.

No one else is scared. You shouldn't be scared, either, I chastised myself. Instead of lessening my terror, it only added shame. *I should be braver than this.*

"We're almost down," Marcus said, concern lacing his voice.

I choked on my teary inhale and hid my face against Oliver.

"Another ten feet. Five feet. Aaand . . . we're down."

The ship lurched. I screamed, short and sharp. Marcus's hand rubbed up and down my spine.

"The ship's going to rock a bit while Patrick unloads bottles and brings more aboard."

Blindly, I straightened. Black dots danced in my vision as I swiped tears from my lashes. Urgency propelled me to my feet, and I squirmed against Oliver's restraint.

"Mika, what—" Marcus asked, but I was already sprinting for the ladder.

With shaking fingers, I tossed the bundle of rope over the railing, then flung myself after it before I lost my nerve. My boots slipped on the hemp rungs, and the coarse rope bit into my palms, but I barely noticed. When my feet hit solid ground, fresh tears sprang to my eyes. I wanted to collapse right there, but a vague awareness of people shuffling around me kept me in motion. Staggering on wobbly knees, I set my sights on a wooden bench against bright white clapboard siding. A shimmer of carnelian red reflected off the building, then Oliver was at my side, his wing keeping me from toppling when I fell to my knees in front of the bench. I grabbed the wooden seat, intending to pull myself up, but I couldn't find the strength. Tears splashed my forearms, and I dropped my head to rest my cheek against the sun-heated wood.

I couldn't do that again. My heart couldn't take it.

Marcus's large hands cupped my shoulders, and he gently lifted me to the bench, seating my trembling body next to his and wrapping an arm around me. Shame burned in my gut, and I feebly scrubbed at the tear tracks on my cheeks. I didn't want to be this woman. I wanted to be strong and competent. Someone Marcus respected. Someone worthy of being called a gargoyle guardian.

Fresh tears filled my vision. Maybe I wasn't cut out to be a guardian. Maybe I was meant to remain a small-time quartz artisan. At least then, I could spend my days safe on the ground.

A train whistle split the air, cutting through my morose

thoughts. A gravel-packed lane wove to my left and right, dividing a bank of squat buildings at the edge of town from the cultivated fields crisscrossing the clear-cut hillside. Dust hazed the air above a winding dirt road farther out, and between rows of cornstalks, I caught glimpses of air carts and horse-drawn wagons meandering toward the town. My gaze snagged on the twin metallic ribbons of train tracks curving southeast, toward Terra Haven. Toward home.

A sick twist of yearning and guilt knotted my gut. If I took the next train, I could be home by dinnertime. The *Happy Hopper* and this entire flight could be nothing more than fuel for tonight's nightmares.

I didn't have enough money for a ticket, but I could borrow some from Marcus—

The fantasy burst into painful shards. Asking Marcus for money would mean announcing, out loud, that I was giving up. It would mean giving in to my cowardice.

Nausea pulsed in my throat, and it had nothing to do with airsickness.

"What happens if the tree blooms before we get there?" I asked, my voice raw.

"Then we'll disembark at Patrick's next stop and get a ride home with the squad when they pass through."

"In another airship?"

Marcus snorted. "For a personal errand? There's no way the captain would spring for that. I'm betting they took the cart. It'll be a cramped ride back for the two of us."

I sat straighter. I had seen the squad's air cart. It couldn't levitate higher than six feet. "What if—" I cleared my throat and flattened my tone, hiding my newfound, traitorous hope. "What if the tree's already bloomed?"

"Not a chance." Marcus smiled and clasped my hands in his. "I sent messages ahead. The tree hasn't bloomed yet. I'll keep checking, but we've all still got a shot at asking the tree a question."

"Oh." So much for an easy out. "Good."

Defeated, I dropped my gaze from Marcus's.

A woman in a Message in a Bottle uniform hustled from the open doors of the single-story warehouse beside us, propelling a crate of bottles ahead of her on cushions of air. Her curious gaze bounced from Oliver leaning against my shins to Marcus, and her footsteps slowed, her pinched expression melting into admiration as her eyes slid up his body.

"Nicole, your messages," Patrick drawled.

The woman jerked to face forward, then righted her listing crate and rushed to the open cargo hold of the *Happy Hopper*, her brown cheeks tinged pink.

"Mika." Marcus squeezed my fingers.

I didn't want to look into his eyes and see pity, so I let my gaze rest on his tan throat. His soft cotton pullover was starting to fray at the collar, and I wondered if it was a favorite, and if we would be dating long enough for me to find out.

"We don't have to keep going," Marcus said.

I peeked at his expression through my lashes. He was serious. He would give up his chance to go to the everlasting tree for me.

I drew in a shaky breath, savoring the bitter scent of sun-heated dandelion stalks and dust.

"How many more stops are there?" I asked. How many more times would I have to endure taking off and landing? How many more chances would we have of crashing and dying?

"A handful. But once we reach the tree, that's it. You won't have to get into another airship for a long time. And who knows. Maybe traveling for days in a cramped cart with the squad will make you miss the freedom of the skies."

"Oh, you'll definitely miss all this," Patrick said, stopping close enough to cast a shadow across my face and pointing both thumbs at his chest. "I didn't get the nickname Mr. Majestic just for my flying skills."

"Ew," Nicole said. "No one calls you that."

"Not to my face, but when I'm gone—"

"You don't want to know what we call you behind your back, scrawny."

"Hey!"

Laughing to herself, Nicole disappeared inside the warehouse.

"Anyway," Patrick said, drawing out the word as he turned back to me. "I'm in the running for pilot of the year, and that comes with a sizable bonus, so you know this ship is going to deliver its cargo intact and on time." Patrick slapped Marcus on the arm. "Speaking of which, we're ahead of schedule but falling behind every second we sit here."

My palms started to sweat. I glanced longingly toward the train station, then down at Oliver. My friend's trusting expression pierced my heart. Would Oliver think so highly of me if he knew how tempted I was to abandon this once-in-a-lifetime opportunity to help gargoyles just to avoid another terrifying flight?

"We'll be right there," Marcus said.

Patrick's gaze dropped to mine, and I glanced away, but not before I saw exasperation tighten the corners of his eyes.

"Don't take too long. I don't want to miss my chance to ask the tree my question."

Marcus waited until Patrick was out of hearing range

before speaking. "So what'll it be? Back to Terra Haven or onward with Mr. Mediocre?"

The nickname wasn't particularly funny, but I managed a smile.

"Onward." My voice wavered, and the acrid taste of panic chased a lump of guilt down my throat when I swallowed. "I'm Mika Stillwater, gargoyle guardian. If I don't use the tree to help gargoyles, I'll regret it forever."

Marcus squeezed my hands and stood. "Can you walk?" he asked.

I bit my lower lip. If I were headed to the train, I could run. But back to the dirigible?

I shook my head.

Marcus scooped me up in his arms. I buried my face in his neck and tried to convince myself he wasn't carrying me to my death.

I hugged Oliver, anchored by his sturdy body coiled around me. Blue sky surrounded us, studded with wispy white clouds. Cringing at every thump and bump, I rode out our ascent on the deck this time. Patrick had assured me fresh air and sunshine would ease my airsickness, and he was right, but the view did nothing to assuage my terror.

A tear slid down my cheek. I wanted to be on the ground. If humans were meant to fly, we would have been born with wings. It was pure hubris that made anyone think a frangible vessel like the *Happy Hopper* and its patchwork spells made us skyworthy.

"How are you feeling?" Marcus asked.

Humiliated. Weak. Terrified, I thought.

"All right," I forced out.

"Do you want to sit on the bench?" Marcus pointed to a bowed slat of wood tacked to the rickety railing. I swallowed a spate of hysterical laughter that bubbled behind barely restrained sobs.

"Here. I want to stay here."

"It's kind of in the—" Patrick protested, but Marcus cut him off.

"Here is fine." He rubbed my back with a warm palm. "Is there anything I can do?"

I shook my head and swiped my wet cheek against my shirtsleeve before giving him a wan smile. "I'm just ready to be at the everlasting tree."

Marcus squeezed my shoulders and rocked onto his heels. "Let me see what I can do to put a bit more speed into this dragger."

"No. That's not what I—"

"Who are you calling a dragger?" Patrick demanded, drowning out my feeble protests.

"We're going what? Seven knots? Eight?" Marcus straightened and raised a hand to test the air.

"More like ten," Patrick said.

Marcus arched a skeptical brow at his friend.

"Would you like me to do the math for you, big guy?" Patrick asked. "I've been flying longer than you've been a fancy-pants FPD man. I know my ship."

"You've gotten complacent. An hour early, an hour late, what does it matter when it's just cargo?"

"It matters to my boss."

"You can always blame it on the air currents. But when something is trying to kill you, you don't have that luxury."

Patrick rolled his eyes. "Oh, here we go. Wise warrior, please show me how you can do it better." He stepped aside with a sweeping bow, as if he were an actor conceding the stage, but when he straightened, he tossed Marcus a rude gesture.

The boards beneath me quivered as Marcus strode across the deck. My fingers spasmed around Oliver, digging into the slender column of his neck. Unaffected by the pressure, Oliver leaned into me and crooned quietly.

"It's all about spells and sails. Watch and learn," Marcus said.

"He wasn't always this obnoxious," Patrick said to me. "It's the FPD. Would you believe Velasquez was as sweet as a baby kitsune and twice as cuddly before he went through training?"

I barely registered his words, my eyes locked on Marcus. He bent over the railing, his head dipping out of sight. When he lifted up on his toes, his torso suspended over nothing, I stopped breathing.

"You're not going to find anything amiss with my spells," Patrick shouted. "I fine-tuned every one of them myself."

"Including the levitation spells?" Marcus asked, stepping away from the railing.

I let out my pent-up breath and soothed my bloodless fingers down Oliver's wing.

"Levitation, propulsion, moisture detection, bindings, the works. I've perfected them all. What do you think I do with my spare time? Practice bird calls?"

"Your levitation spells are adding drag that's forcing the *Hopper* to fly at a cant."

"That's absurd!" Patrick narrowed his eyes and stomped to the railing. I looked away when he folded himself over the side and hung by his arm strength alone.

"Do you see it?" Marcus asked.

"I think you're blowing wind up my pantaloons," Patrick yelled, his voice muffled from his precarious perch.

"What about now?" Magic flowed from Marcus, a complex weave of air, water, and fire that dove over the edge and out of sight.

"That's not going to work, because you can't— Wait! You're going to—"

Patrick's voice cut off abruptly. Horror catapulted my stomach into my throat, but a quick glance confirmed he hadn't fallen overboard. Somehow the pilot clung to the railing with a single fist and one hooked ankle, the rest of him dangling out of sight.

A frightening series of pops and moans rang through the ship. I clutched Oliver, fully expecting the boards beneath us to give way and drop us to our deaths.

Patrick's feet thumped to the deck. "Damn your hairy testi— Ahem, pardon, Mika and Oliver." He clapped Marcus on the shoulder. "Velasquez, you fiery phoenix. You just got propulsion from the levitation spells."

"It's not much."

"It shouldn't be possible at all."

"Are you sure it's safe?" I asked. Messing with the levitation spells while this far above solid ground seemed like the epitome of idiocy.

"In this balmy weather?" Patrick lifted a hand toward the open sky. "Safe as soup." He strode around me and Oliver to the front of the ship. There, he fondly patted the railing, leaning close to whisper, "Do you like being the fastest little ship in the sky?"

I turned to Marcus, bewildered. "Is soup safe?"

"I didn't make any changes the *Happy Hopper* can't handle," Marcus assured me. "Now to fix the wings."

"What's wrong with the wings?" I cast a frantic glance toward the sails. Sometime after takeoff, Patrick had snapped them open, and the taut canvases now splayed to either side of the ship, supported by frail wooden frames.

"Nothing's wrong with the *Hopper*'s wings," Patrick said.

"They're a foot too long," Marcus said.

"They're regulation length. Message in a Bottle engineers designed them for optimum efficiency."

"A bit shorter, and we could squeeze another two or three knots out of the propulsion spells."

Patrick planted his hands on his hips. Marcus folded his arms across his chest and waited.

"You're that sure of yourself?" Patrick finally asked.

Marcus nodded.

"You're a cocky bastard, you know that?" Patrick asked.

"I told you, I've had to learn how to make adjustments on the fly. This will be easy." Marcus strode to the side of the ship.

"Wait! You're not going to do it *now*, are you?" I asked.

"Patrick, when is the next stop?"

Patrick cupped a hand over his eyes, studying the horizon. "At this rate, another three hours or so."

"If I fix the wings, we can shave thirty minutes off that." Marcus turned to me. "I'm not going to let you miss the everlasting tree by a few hours because our ship was too slow."

"But . . ." Dumbfounded, I fumbled for words. Marcus stood at the railing, the drop yawning in front of him. The danger should have been obvious.

"Trust me, I've got this," he said.

I transferred my incredulous stare to Patrick. He shrugged.

"I can fix anything he messes up."

Was that supposed to be reassuring?

Marcus vaulted the railing and landed on the wing. It creaked under his weight, and the ship tipped fractionally in his direction. My heart clawed up my throat, choking me. Crouching slightly, Marcus let go of the railing and wobbled. I stopped breathing, holding myself motionless, as if my own rigidity could anchor Marcus.

My daredevil boyfriend took a cautious step. The wooden beam beneath him groaned.

"Will the wing hold him?" I rasped, flicking a glance toward Patrick.

He gave me another shrug. "I guess we'll see."

Oliver sat up straighter, tracking Marcus's progress.

"Shouldn't you link with him?" I asked.

"Why? He's got Oliver's boost."

If I could have moved, I would have shaken Patrick. Hard. The useless pilot stood five feet from me, his arms crossed and his eyes narrowed as he watched Marcus take on this foolhardy risk. Mentally cursing the stupidity of all men, but especially two men in particular, I took a stab at Patrick's pride.

"This is your ship. Are you just going to stand there and let Marcus mutilate it?"

Patrick chuckled and shook his head. "All joking aside, I trust Velasquez. He knows what he's doing."

"I'm sure he does," I ground out. "But shouldn't these types of alterations wait until we land?"

"You're not worried, are you?"

I couldn't believe I had to spell this out for him. "The man I love is perched over his own death with no safety net. Do you know how to create a spell like that? A safety net? We could link, and with Oliver's boost, we should be strong enough to catch Marcus when—if—he falls."

Patrick's eyes widened. "Oh, you're for real. Most women enjoy Velasquez's swagger. All that muscle and might tends to make you gals—"

I gathered a balance of elements and thrust it toward Patrick. He raised his hands in defense, as if I were attacking him, not trying to initiate a link.

"It's not necessary, Mika," Patrick soothed, his tone

unexpectedly sympathetic. "Velasquez can be a true idiot sometimes, but not about things like that." He flicked a finger to indicate the wing. "I don't know how long you've known him, but he's as good with the elements as he boasts. He can walk on air—literally. Just look for yourself."

I jerked to face Marcus—and promptly lost control of my magic. The elements imploded with a small pop.

Marcus knelt on the empty space in front of the wing. A paper-thin shelf of solidified air supported his muscular bulk, and a delicate spell attached his fragile platform to the wing, keeping him moving—floating—with the airship. With no regard to the chasm beneath him, Marcus cinched the wing's bindings, yanking far too hard on the ropes criss-crossing the canvas for my comfort. The wing creaked and groaned, sending a shudder through the deck. Black dots danced in my vision.

"Breathe," Oliver murmured.

I sucked in a breath. Marcus knotted the binding into a tighter configuration and stood, eyeing his modifications. The wing dipped and rebounded over a pocket of unstable air, bouncing Marcus. My heart lodged in my throat. Marcus bent his knees and rode the gyrations as easily as if he were standing on the ground. Then he glanced over at me and waved.

I wanted to strangle him.

To Marcus, this was a game. A dirigible flight across the country didn't register as dangerous to him, just like perching atop a scrap of magic thousands of feet above the ground didn't strike him as risky. It wasn't Marcus's fault that his bravery far outstripped mine.

It was part of the reason I had fallen for him. He was spontaneous, strong, commanding, and confident—all traits I lacked. Any moment now, he would see it, and our fragile new relationship would wither away. How could he continue to love someone who couldn't even summon the bravery to stand on a dirigible's deck, let alone approach the railing and dance on the wing?

Marcus swung over the railing and jogged to my side. Relief weakened my spine, and I soaked in the sight of him safely back on the semi-solid planks of the deck.

"See what I mean?" Marcus asked. "The airflow is smoother."

"Marginally," Patrick agreed. "But now we're flying crooked."

"Let me fix that."

The deck boards vibrated in tandem with the thump of Marcus's steps, then stilled when he sprang onto the opposite wing.

"Nothing bad will happen to him. I promise," Patrick said.

I nodded. Patrick awkwardly patted my shoulder, then walked away. I hunched around Oliver, wishing this whole trip was over instead of having barely begun. I didn't want to watch Marcus flirt with death on the end of the wing, but I couldn't make myself look away, either. I was afraid that without my gaze to tether him, he would fall.

My pulse pounded when Marcus tilted forward to force slack into the ropes that secured the canvas to its frame, and I forgot to breathe when he wrestled the wingtip into a new, shorter shape. Finally, he straightened. Marcus walked halfway back to the deck, then inexplicably stopped and turned to face the front of the ship.

I whipped around, expecting a cliff or wyvern in our path. Empty blue sky stretched across the horizon. When I spun back to Marcus, his arms were spread wide. Wind ruffled his short black hair. Sunlight glinted off his grin. He crafted a quick amplification spell and shouted into it. "You should see the view from here, Mika. It's like having wings."

My spine snapped rigid. Phantom pain flared across my shoulder blades where fresh carnelian scars bisected my skin.

In a fugue state, saturated with the inhuman power of a gargoyle baetyl, I had given those scars to myself in an attempt to grow wings into my own flesh. Because beneath my terror of heights, I yearned to fly. Naturally. Gracefully. Like Oliver. *With* Oliver.

Anguish tore through raw emotional scabs, lacerating me anew. Severing the wings from my back and returning to this landlocked, inferior form had broken me. It had saved my life, too, but the loss haunted me.

Marcus knew this. Days earlier, he had witnessed the baetyl's majestic power when it nearly consumed me, and he had been the one to piece me back together after its loss.

Closing my eyes, I focused on breathing past the fiery coal embedded in my chest. The ship shuddered. I pressed my face into Oliver's neck as the wind shoved harder against me, tugging the last of my hair from its scraggly braid.

The deck vibrated, announcing Marcus's return to relative safety. I opened my eyes to find him lounging beside me, as if he were on a picnic, not fresh from a death-defying stunt. The prideful grin on his face hardened my anger into a knot beneath my breastbone.

"Did you see me out there? It took a bit of muscling to get those wings into shape." Marcus rubbed a flexed bicep, inviting me to admire his brawn.

"I saw." My voice cracked over the words, anger and pain raw in my tone, and I hated it. Tipping my chin toward Patrick, I asked, "Water, please?"

Silence lengthened behind my question. I kept my gaze

directed toward Patrick's leather boots. Finally, the pilot slid a bottle into my hand. I clutched it and took a swig. Oliver's tail twitched nervously. In my peripheral vision, I saw Patrick mouth something to Marcus, then shrug.

"How are you feeling, Mika?" Marcus asked.

"Fine."

The lie may as well have been a slap the way Marcus stiffened. His gaze darted to Oliver, then Patrick. The pilot shook his head and backed away. After two steps, he spun and hastened to the rear of the ship, abandoning Marcus to his fate.

4

Slowly, using more caution than he had shown when traipsing along the *Hopper*'s wing, Marcus leveraged himself into a seated position.

"Are you angry with me?" he asked.

My gaze snapped to his, and I let him see the fury burning inside me. He flinched, but the confusion in his expression forced my words out even as they choked me.

"That was a stupid risk."

"Fixing the wings? It wasn't risky for—"

"You could have died."

"Whoa, Mika . . ." Marcus started to reach for me, but he dropped his hand to his knee without touching me. "I was never in danger. You said you wanted more speed—"

"No. You heard what you wanted to hear."

Oliver whined and tightened his wing across my legs in a stony hug. I stroked a hand down his spine, but I doubted he found my trembling touch soothing.

"I didn't—" Marcus cut himself off and took a deep breath, frustration apparent in the bunching of his jaw. "You're right. I want to make it to the tree before it blooms.

We both do. And I was never in danger. I'm sorry I scared you, but I thought if I showed you how safe this airship is, you would be less . . . You would be more relaxed."

Less scared, he meant to say. I gritted my teeth. Was this the future of our relationship? Marcus the Brave comforting Mika the Cowardly? I didn't want to be terrified of heights. I didn't want to be scared of flying. I didn't want Marcus to think he had to fix me, and I didn't want to feel like I needed to be fixed.

"You know my job," he continued. "Balancing on a dirigible's wing doesn't even rank among the risky situations I've been in this month." Marcus's blue eyes searched mine. Tentatively, he reached for me, this time resting his hand atop mine, stilling me. "I don't get it. How is this different? I mean, *you've* engaged in far more risky feats than standing on a dirigible's wing." His thumb stroked the back of my hand, where a line of amethyst hexagon scars trailed from my pinkie to my wrist—another souvenir of the baetyl and a reminder of how close I had come to dying.

"That was different," I said. "We were saving lives. It was for a purpose."

"Getting to the everlasting tree could save more lives."

Oliver rubbed his cool muzzle against my cheek, his breath stirring my hair. His gentleness melted the hard knot inside me.

I lifted my gaze from the beautiful amethyst scars, tears filling my eyes. "It's like having wings?" I whispered. A tear spilled onto my cheek and rushed toward my chin. "Really?"

Marcus cursed and surged toward me, wrapping an arm around my back, bringing the other to my cheek to gently wipe away the next tear. "Oh, Mika, I'm such an ass. I didn't think. I shouldn't have said that."

I shook my head and hid my face against Marcus's neck.

He squeezed his arms around me, scooting closer to hug me around Oliver.

"I'm sorry," Marcus whispered, his breath stirring my hair.

His words, his embrace, his affection soothed the fragile bandage back in place across the ache in my chest, buffering me from the pain of my severed connection to the baetyl. The rawness of my loss receded, and my tears dried. Abashed, I sat back. I had to look a fright, my face blotchy from crying and flushed with embarrassment, my hair a snarl. I wasn't making a great impression on Patrick, either, though I couldn't bring myself to care. It was Marcus's opinion I worried the most about, but my self-consciousness faded when I found only tenderness in his expression. He placed a gentle kiss on my lips, then another. Warmth kindled in my chest and spiraled through my stomach, and I leaned into the next kiss with more enthusiasm.

"Did I ever show you the scar I got when I was dating the gryphon rider in Lychee Valley?" Patrick asked loudly. "It's right here on my left cheek." He spun around and grabbed the waistband of his pants.

"Whoa! No! Keep your pants on," Marcus said, shielding my eyes with his hand. Reaching around me, he cupped his free hand over Oliver's eyes, too.

"Oh, I thought we were showing each other things we didn't want to see."

"You are such a child," Marcus grumbled, dropping his hands. He sat back with obvious irritation, his lips twisted into a near pout. It was oddly endearing, and I found myself smiling for the first time since boarding the *Happy Hopper*.

The dirigible jounced over rough air, knocking my knees against the underside of Oliver's wing. My stomach constricted. I located the distant horizon and locked my gaze on it, breathing slow and deep.

"Have you decided what you're going to ask the everlasting tree?" Marcus asked.

How I can make sure I never, ever have to fly again, I almost said, but I could tell Marcus was attempting to distract me, so I swallowed my sarcasm. "I'm still working on my wording."

"I know what I'm asking," Patrick said. "It's real simple: 'Where can I find loads of money?'"

"You can ask the everlasting tree *anything*, and you want to ask it about money?" Marcus scoffed.

"No. I want to ask it about *loads* of money." Patrick walked along the railing, testing the ropes connecting the airship to the balloon and reinforcing the bindings with twists of earth element. "With loads of money, I could do anything."

"It's still a dumb use of your question." The words were out of my mouth before I realized how rude they were.

"Really? You're going to insult the man keeping you afloat?" Patrick left off examining the ship and turned to face me.

"Well, I mean, I—"

"No, be honest. Tell me how you really feel." Patrick crossed his arms.

I darted a glance at Marcus, wishing I'd kept my mouth shut.

"Use small words," Marcus said. "It'll be easier for him to understand."

"You're not going to convince me my question isn't brilliant," Patrick said.

"Perhaps if you got a direct answer from the tree," I

agreed. "But you get a magic-made clue, one that may take you years to decipher."

According to the articles Kylie had written as part of her special assignment covering the everlasting tree's blooming, receiving a seed was only the beginning. By all historical accounts, most seeds evolved many times before the recipient unlocked their final answer—if they ever did. "You might find your *loads* of money minutes before you die. Then what good will it do you?"

Patrick opened his mouth, then clicked it shut, his eyes narrowing.

"But you don't really want money," I continued.

"Oh no, you're wrong. I really do want money."

"You want what you can buy with money," I countered. "Which is what?"

Patrick gestured expansively. "Many things. I want to visit every continent before I die and see all the wonders of the world. I want to fall in love with a different woman in every country. I want to fly a thousand different types of ships. I want to eat exotic foods and wear clothes that aren't..." He plucked at his distasteful uniform. "That aren't *this*. Basically, I want the freedom to go where I want, when I want, and do what I want, and I need money for that. A lot of money."

"Or you need to word your question better."

"It's just that simple, is it? How would you fit all that into a single question?"

"You have to work with the tree's magic. The everlasting tree gives you a seed, and it's up to you to follow its clues to your answer." Petting a hand down Oliver's sun-warmed neck, I carefully shifted to a more comfortable position beneath the security of his wing. My gaze snagged on the blue sky behind Patrick, and my stomach tried to fold in on itself at the reminder of how high up we were.

Magic spooled from the pilot, disappearing into spells beneath the ship, making adjustments I didn't want to contemplate. I forced myself to keep talking, using the distraction Marcus had given me to hold my terror at bay. "The trick, I think, is to ask a question that might not have a final answer. From what it sounds like, you want to travel, Patrick. Does it matter to you if you do it with thousands of dollars in your pockets? Or is the travel enough? Maybe you want to ask the tree how you can have a grand adventure that spans all the continents, or how you can fly every airship in existence in your life."

Patrick squinted at me as if seeing me for the first time. "You know, you might be onto something there, Mika. Perhaps, 'How can I seduce a woman on every continent in every airship?'"

"You're definitely going to need new apparel for that."

"Mmm, good point. 'How can I seduce a woman on every continent in every airship while looking debonair?'"

"It's getting a bit wordy," Marcus said. "Maybe, 'How can I see the world without annoying any women?'"

Patrick shook his head, nibbling on the side of his lip. "Too impractical. Besides, sometimes annoying a woman is part of the fun. It adds to the tension." He winked at me.

I rolled my eyes.

"Seriously, it's like your brain never evolved past the age of twelve," Marcus said.

"Fortunately, my body is all man." Patrick flexed his wiry arms and puffed out his chest.

I ducked my face so he couldn't see my smirk, not wanting to encourage any further displays of his manhood.

Marcus ran his callused palm down my bare forearm.

Goosebumps chased his touch. "Back to you," he said. "What are you going to ask the tree?"

"I want to help as many gargoyles as possible."

"Shocking," Marcus teased.

His lapis lazuli eyes glowed like gems in his tan face, his gentle humor and affection shining in their depths. I leaned closer, enchanted. When I stared into his mesmerizing eyes, the riot of anxiety inside me quieted. Even the air around us felt calmer. Too calm.

A bolt of panic shot through me, chased a second later by logic: We hadn't stalled. Marcus had erected a windproof bubble around the three of us, protecting us from the cool gusts buffeting the *Happy Hopper*'s deck. Snuggled against Oliver, with Marcus relaxed next to me, I could almost pretend we were sitting on the porch at home instead of thousands of feet in the air.

"I'm a guardian, just one person, and there are so many gargoyles," I said, forcing my thoughts back on track before my brain fixated on the enormous void beneath us and how quickly our fragile, unnatural travel through the invisible currents could go wrong. "I don't know how to find all the gargoyles who might need my help, or even how to let gargoyles know I'm here for them."

"Every gargoyle in Terra Haven knows who you are," Oliver said.

"Thanks to you."

Even before I knew what a gargoyle guardian *was*, Oliver recognized the ability in me and had announced my title to every gargoyle he met. But in-person introductions weren't enough. Gargoyle guardians weren't common. As far as I knew, I was the only one in the state, possibly the only one this side of the Mississippi River.

"But what about gargoyles outside Terra Haven? Are

there gargoyles in need out there, in the countryside, in the towns we're flying past?" I gestured to the world below us, keeping my other hand flat against Oliver, not quite ready to release him completely. "How can I know when I'm needed? Which is what I want to ask the tree, only in a way it can't directly answer. If I get the question right, my seed can be my guide, taking me to a gargoyle in need, then evolving to take me to the next one, and the next, indefinitely."

Marcus's eyebrows rose. "That's ambitious . . . and really smart." He brushed my arm again, leaving his hand resting on my wrist.

Tension seeped from my spine. At some point, I had stopped jumping and twitching at every creak of the dirigible's ropes. The pounding of my pulse against my eardrums had receded, and I could hear birds calling to each other, their cries muffled by Marcus's windproof spell.

We're safe, I told myself, almost believing it this time.

"You're going to do incredible things with your seed," Marcus said. His thumb brushed lightly across the back of my hand, stroking the amethyst scars. "Or I should say, *more* incredible things."

"I hope so." I sat a little straighter and breathed a little easier.

"Keep it evolving into new answers," Patrick said, pacing at the front of the ship. "That's not just smart, Mika, that's brilliant. I need to figure out how to get the tree to guide me from wonder to wonder. Wonders with lush lips and long legs and full bre—"

Marcus cleared his throat.

"Full, ah, full berths." Patrick shot me a sheepish glance, then ruined it with a lascivious eyebrow waggle. "I want my seed to give me lots of *airships* to pick from."

"Of course." I turned aside to hide my smile. Sunlight

shimmered across my face, fracturing off something shiny. I squinted, shading my eyes with my hand.

The sky wavered and flexed.

Water, my brain translated.

Alarm shot down my spine, and I seized Oliver with both hands. Without moving the wing I held in a death grip, Oliver reared onto his hind legs, stretching to see over the railing. A lake shimmered in the sunlight, almost level with our ship. Which meant—

I spun toward the bow, expecting to see the ground rushing toward us, but empty blue sky wrapped the ship. The deck remained flat.

"What is that?" Oliver asked.

Marcus was already on his feet, a hand lifted to shade his eyes. "An awanyu aerie."

I squirmed out from under Oliver, kneeling next to him. I wasn't brave enough to let go of him, but I had to see this.

A sphere of water five times the size of the *Happy Hopper* floated like a jewel in the cloudless sky. Nebulous shadows stirred within it, distorted into obscurity by the curve of the globe's outer edge and the blur of air and water elements whipping around the suspended lake, keeping it afloat. Sparkles of silver and copper glinted in the sunlight as awanyus leapt across the water's surface. Magic vibrated in the wake of each horned serpent's appearance, strengthening the elemental vortex around the water.

"What are awanyus?" Oliver glanced from the liquid aerie to me and back.

"Water wyrms," I said. I'd heard of them but had never seen one outside of illustrations in books. "They migrate south in swarms during the summer, carrying their young in these massive levitated lakes. Every couple of days, they drop into local waters, feed and rest, then carry on. They travel thousands of miles to Axixic, and in the fall, they return north once the babies are strong enough to handle the icy temperatures."

"They also stir up unpredictable air currents," Patrick said, jogging to the rear of the *Hopper* to tinker with the rigging. "We're lucky this is a young aerie. The babies aren't contributing much to the overall magic. Give them another month, month and a half, and this aerie will generate some impressive monsoons."

I tightened my grip on Oliver and eyed the *Hopper*'s balloon, which creaked against the ropes netting it. More than before? Just in case, I gathered an even balance of the elements, prepared to link with Marcus if he needed the extra magic. I reminded myself he already had Oliver's boost to aid him, which was more reassuring. My magical abilities skewed heavily toward earth, specifically quartz, neither of which was of much use on an aircraft.

"Let's fly wide," Marcus said.

"I made course corrections ten minutes ago when I first spotted it." Patrick adjusted a handle at the tail of the ship and nudged air element toward a spell attached to the balloon. "It's coming up on us fast but is angled more southward. We should fall behind it by half a mile or more."

"Are you looking to draft off the aerie?" Marcus asked.

"That's the plan."

"Is that wise?" I asked.

"The wyrms don't care about us," Marcus said. "So long as we keep our distance, they probably won't even notice us. Using a bit of their magic to boost our flight won't harm them or us."

A menagerie of birds swooped around the aerie, drawn to the floating buffet. Opportunistic gulls circled beneath the orb, diving for displaced fish knocked from the swirling waters, while smaller belted kingfishers used the spin of the wyrms' magic to skim beneath the surface and shoot back out with fish in their beaks.

All the birds scattered at the repetitious cry of an incoming osprey. Arrowing through the sky, the white-chested raptor slammed into the aerie. It flashed through the whirlwind of magic, disappearing for a second before surging out of the water, a squirming copper wyrm hardly longer than my palm in its talons. The baby awanyu whipped about wildly, buffeting the osprey with a frenzy of air and water elements. Droplets sprayed from the bird's wings and shattered under the magical onslaught, anatomizing into a heavy mist. Engulfed, the osprey struggled to free itself, but it was too slow.

A seething mass of adult awanyus converged beneath it, riling up their magic into a froth. Water bulged from the sphere, swallowing the osprey's talons and the young serpent it clutched. With a frustrated cry, the osprey folded its wings and dropped free of the awanyus' elemental vortex, escaping empty-taloned.

My stomach fell with the bird, and I yanked my gaze up before vertigo could induce nausea. Sitting back on my heels, I stroked Oliver's wing to ground myself. Inside the aerie, the awanyus darted into motion, spinning away from the attack site, their magic rippling across the water's surface to keep it in motion.

A pulse of energy tapped against my thoughts, so faint that my anxiety and curiosity had masked it when it first came into range. A gargoyle flew in the sky with us.

I craned my head to peer over the railing. Sensing gargoyles was a new ability for me, a side effect of melding with the ancient, semi-sentient gargoyle hatching site—or perhaps it was the baetyl's version of a parting gift. Since that fateful day, Oliver's presence existed inside my head as a bundle of energy, currently made large by his proximity. Even if it were pitch black and I wasn't clinging to him like my life depended on it, I could have pointed straight to him. The same was true of any gargoyle in my vicinity.

"Do you sense the gargoyle?" I asked Oliver, keeping my voice low so it wouldn't carry beyond the two of us.

Oliver scanned the sky, a new intensity in his body language. "I don't . . . Yes, there!" He reared onto his hind feet, yanking my arm in its socket as he rose.

I shifted my grip to the tip of his wing, testing the knot of energy in my head. It wasn't moving fast enough to be flying, but it wasn't stationary, either. Ever so slowly, it was approaching . . .

Horror broke through me, the obvious conclusion delayed by my desire to deny it.

"There's a gargoyle in the aerie," Oliver shouted.

I strained to spot the gargoyle in the swirl of water and wyrms, but the frothing, wobbling surface of the flying lake warped and refracted the sun's light, providing only vague impressions of lumpy shadows in the water's depths.

"Are you certain?" Marcus asked.

"Yes," I said.

Marcus searched my eyes. Aside from Oliver, he was the only person who knew of my newfound ability.

"And it's alive?" he asked.

"Yes." Fear closed my throat around the word. Gargoyles couldn't breathe underwater.

I prodded the energy in my head, testing it as best I could. It felt weak, far too weak for how close we were to the aerie. The awanyus' magic was powerful enough to keep tons of water afloat, but the spells swirling around the surface weren't designed to cage a gargoyle. Gravity alone should have pulled the stone creature free.

"Something must be holding her. Or him. Trapping them," I said. "We need to get closer."

"That's not a good idea," Patrick said. "You thought the turbulence was bad during takeoff. If we get too close . . ." He trailed off as I shoved myself to my feet.

"We don't have a choice." I braced myself against Oliver's solid frame, my eyes locked on the aerie. "Take us closer."

5

"I don't think—"

I flicked my gaze to Patrick, and his mouth snapped shut.

"Closer," I repeated.

I forced myself to take a step toward the railing. It felt as if I were balancing atop a fragile raft, each step poised to upset the ship's delicate balance and capsize us. It didn't matter that I had seen the men jog across these same boards. My brain refused to accept that my movements wouldn't become the catalyst of our demise.

But I needed a better view, and that meant trekking to the railing. Or at least, nearer to the railing.

"Sheesh. She's got that scary look down better than you, Velasquez," Patrick whispered. "I didn't think that was possible. And now I get it, because before, I was wondering how Mr. Badass ended up with someone so—"

"Shut it," Marcus snapped. Magic shot from him, diving into the spells around the ship.

"Ah, there's the growly Velasquez we all know and love," Patrick grumbled, guiding his magic with Marcus's.

Oliver inched along beside me, holding one wing high and steady for me to clutch. Cool wind gusted across the deck, lifting my hair from my neck and chasing goose bumps down my arms. Intent on the dirigible's spells, Marcus had let his sheltering cocoon of still air dissipate. The *Hopper* tilted, turning on a tight axis toward the aerie. I froze, legs splayed wide, my stomach shoving my heart into my throat. When the ship stabilized, I forced myself to take another two steps, but my feet took root when I was still an arm's length from the railing. My breathing huffed choppily at my throat. I swallowed and kept my eyes locked on the aerie, refusing to glance down at the ground so terribly far away.

Suspended in the sky, without another object to compare it to, the aerie's size had deceived me. It wasn't merely a few times larger than our dirigible; it could easily swallow several city blocks. Wind kicked off the aerie, arcing rainbow-adorned sprays of mist dozens of feet into the air. The deck gyrated in the turbulent air, the wings creaking from the added strain.

"This is a weak aerie?" I asked.

"We're about two hundred yards away, maybe a little more, and we're only now feeling its winds." Marcus adjusted a propulsion spell before he continued. "If this were an aerie of adults in a fall migration, we would have been forced to land as soon as we spotted them on the horizon."

"I still can't see beneath the surface," Oliver said, rising onto his hind legs again. "It's too murky. Maybe if I fly closer, I can get a better look."

My fingers spasmed around his wing, a denial on the tip of my tongue.

"It's safer for me than the airship," he said.

"Oliver's right." Marcus strode to my side and took my free hand. Weaves of fire and air spun from him to the spells attached to the ship as he spoke, and the *Hopper* steadied. "We need to know what's going on inside the aerie, and it's going to take us another ten minutes to get close."

My stomach knotted. The energy signature of the trapped gargoyle hadn't gotten noticeably stronger with our approach. The gargoyle had to be fighting for their life—and running out of time. They could hold their breath only so long.

I released Oliver, my fingers lingering to stroke the glassy texture of his feathers. "Be quick but careful."

"I promise."

"Approach from above. It will make for easier flying," Marcus said.

Oliver nodded. My heart leapt with my gargoyle over the railing, dropping with him until he snapped his wings open and soared higher. He gained altitude fast, disappearing behind the dirigible's balloon. I tracked his progress in my head. His energy signature diminished as he flew, but it was nowhere close to the size of the trapped gargoyle's.

I prayed we weren't too late.

Oliver reappeared above the aerie, his carnelian wings spread to slow his momentum as he glided over the floating lake. His head hung low, his long, slender body undulating gently with his wings' subtle movement. When he neared the front rim of the aerie, Oliver's feet clenched tight to his body.

"No!" I lunged forward, forgetting about the thousand-foot drop beyond the railing. Marcus's hand brought me up short. By then it was too late.

Oliver folded his wings and dove into the aerie.

The awanyus' magic flared around him. Beneath the

surface, copper serpents scattered. The spinning water splashed against Oliver's stone body, spraying high into the air before swallowing him whole.

His boost winked out. The aerie's surface bowed, then flowed back into motion, as if Oliver had never disturbed it.

"What happened? Why can't I feel—" I froze. I *could* still feel Oliver. He was there, inside my head, a bright knot of energy the same as it had been before he disappeared. "Why can't I feel his boost?"

"The awanyus' magic dampens the elements," Marcus said, his tone clinical and distant, as if he were reciting from a textbook. Only his eyes revealed his concern as he scanned the water's surface. "To keep their aerie intact, the wyrms generate massive amounts of air and water. It muffles the other elements but creates an ideal environment for the baby awanyus. It also discourages other elemental water creatures from hitching a ride in their aeries and feasting on the young when they're at their most vulnerable."

This was the awanyus at their most vulnerable? I couldn't remember much else about the species, not when all my energy was directed at silently urging Oliver to escape, but the fortifications of the aerie were plenty impressive.

A bright knot of crimson broke from the bottom of the aerie. Oliver's boost boomed inside me, and I grabbed greedily for more magic. A river of water poured after him. I didn't take a full breath until he flared his wings and escaped the deluge. Seconds later, the awanyus plugged the gap. Oliver flapped heavily, shedding water as he climbed. I wanted to run to the bow for a better look, but I caught sight of the toylike forest below, and my knees threatened to collapse. Marcus tightened his grip, pulling me against his solid chest.

"A ship!" Oliver landed with enough force to rock the deck. Message bottles rattled alarmingly beneath our feet, and Patrick cursed. Oliver paid neither any attention. "Inside. Caught. Humans and a gargoyle. They can't get out. The humans have spells helping them all breathe, but their magic is weak."

"What's holding the gargoyle?" I asked, pulling away from Marcus to kneel in front of Oliver.

"Loyalty."

It took a second, but I put together the longer answer. If the gargoyle abandoned the ship and its inhabitants, the humans' magic wouldn't be strong enough to maintain their breathing spells. But if they didn't escape soon, everyone would perish.

"What type of ship?" Marcus asked.

"Bigger than this, but it doesn't have a balloon."

"Spells?"

"None that are working."

"How many humans?"

"I felt five but only saw two. The ones inside the ship weren't moving."

Marcus and Patrick exchanged a grim look.

"Should I go back? The humans needed my boost. They were able to strengthen their spells, but I'm not sure how much longer they can hold on."

I glanced up at Marcus, torn between my need to help the trapped gargoyle—and their human companions, of course—and wanting to keep Oliver safe.

"Not yet." Marcus studied the aerie, then me. Determination defined the tension in his broad jaw and flattened his lips into a familiar battle-ready expression, but uncertainty lurked in the depths of his eyes.

His uncharacteristic hesitation sent a chill down my

legs, and I pushed unsteadily to my feet. The deck shook beneath my boot soles, and wind whipping across the railing shoved at my balance. I planted my feet wider.

"What do we do?"

The faintest smile curved the corners of Marcus's lips, and his eyes cleared. "We rescue them."

"You have a spell to part awanyu magic?" Patrick asked, skepticism clear in his tone.

"I've got something better. Take us higher." Marcus sprinted below deck without further explanation.

"Damn it, this isn't what I agreed to," Patrick said, but he rushed to the rear of the ship, magic pulsing from him into the balloon.

The *Hopper* swooped upward. My stomach stayed in place. Lightheaded, I reached blindly for Oliver, and he thrust a wing into my grip.

"Tell me about the gargoyle," I said, gritting my teeth to quell the fear that made them want to chatter.

"He's small, about half my size. Older. Toward the front of the ship, I think. I didn't get as good of a look as I wanted. The awanyus' magic is disorienting. They weren't afraid of me. A few knocked me around. If not for you, I would have lost my sense of direction completely."

I always thought Oliver kept tabs on my location through the boost he shared with me, but the awanyus' magic had prevented that. Did he mean he could sense me like he could sense other gargoyles? Like I could sense him?

Before I could ask, Marcus thundered up the stairs from below, coils of thick rope hanging from his shoulders.

"No way." Patrick raised his hands defensively. "Not a chance. And who is going to tie it? Those tired idiots? *Me?*"

"The pilot stays with the ship," Marcus said.

Patrick deflated fractionally, but his head continued to shake in denial. "It's crazy. Delusional. Impossible."

Marcus snorted. "Hardly."

I glanced back and forth between the men, dread pooling low in my gut. "We *all* stay with the ship," I said. "Right, Marcus?"

"I can't free the trapped ship from here with magic." Marcus tossed a coil of rope to Patrick, heaving the heavy line as if it weighed no more than my bag of seed crystals.

Patrick caught it with a grunt, whipping air around the rope to help support its weight. Marcus jogged to the front of the ship and tested the railing with a violent shove. It creaked. He shook his head, then formed a spinning blade of fire and plunged it into the deck. I slapped a hand over my mouth to stifle a scream. Marcus wielded fire with precision, and he wouldn't do anything to endanger us. But trust was hard when he was poking holes in the only surface between us and certain death.

"You're explaining that to my boss," Patrick said.

"I'll write up a special note on FPD letterhead," Marcus said. "You'll come out sounding like a saint. Now hurry."

Patrick pivoted toward the rear of the ship, shouting to be heard over the rising wind. "I'm only doing this because I'm such a good friend."

"I'm only asking because you're an even better pilot."

"Damn straight." Still muttering under his breath, Patrick hustled across the *Hopper*.

Marcus layered wood and earth around the borehole, sealing the punctured wood with magic. Then he leaned over the railing and proceeded to cut two more holes into the front edge of the ship.

"Marcus?" I wanted reassurances I knew weren't coming, but being in the dark was worse.

He knelt in front of the first hole and spoke without looking at me. "Typically, we would send down a line and pull each person out individually, but I don't think we have that kind of time."

I frowned at the rope in his hands, which he fed through the three holes he had made, then twisted into a complicated knot. At the other end of the ship, Patrick was doing the same with his rope, though he wasn't as fast as Marcus. He kept pausing to pet the deck, as if soothing an injured animal.

"What's that for, then?" I asked.

"For the whole ship."

"The whole . . ." My voice squeezed to nothing as I grasped his plan. He wanted to tie the trapped ship to ours and lift the whole thing out. Patrick had figured it out immediately, and he had assumed— "Wait. You're going into the aerie?"

"Yes."

"But—" My brain caught up with my alarm. Marcus was a trained Federal Pentagon Defense warrior. If anyone was capable of navigating an awanyu aerie and rescuing trapped people, it was him. I didn't want it to be him. I didn't want him to put himself in danger. But he was the gargoyle's and those people's best chance.

Marcus enveloped the knot with a weave of wood, fusing the rope to the *Hopper* as surely as if it had grown from the planks. Then he rose and took my hands.

"I'm going, and so are you."

"*What?*"

"This is a two-person job. If you knew anything about flying an airship or had the strength with air to hold this tub steady, you'd be staying on the *Hopper*. But you don't, so you're coming with me."

"I can't levitate." Stating the obvious was important, because Marcus wasn't making sense. The aerie floated on wild, animal-driven magic. It was suspended an impossible distance above the ground. Marcus said it dampened magic, which meant my weaker abilities would be even less useful inside the aerie than they were aboard the *Hopper*.

"But you can swim. It'll be easier without those boots, too."

I stared blindly at my feet. I wore FPD-worthy boots. The soles were thick, the leather supple but sturdy, and the laces nearly unbreakable. They also weighed a couple of pounds when dry.

Marcus touched my chin, applying gentle pressure until I met his eyes. I could feel the panic in my expression, but I couldn't hide it. Not that I had been doing a stellar job of fooling anyone with my nonexistent bravery on this flight.

"If I could do this without you, I would, but speed is critical. I'm sorry. I know this is scary." His thumb stroked my cheek. Something close to guilt or remorse flashed through his eyes before he masked it. "And I know you can do this. You know why? Because that gargoyle needs you."

I drew in a deep breath, feeling as if I hadn't inhaled in the last five minutes.

"I'll be right beside you," Oliver promised.

Marcus shook his head before Oliver finished his sentence. "Patrick is going to need you up here."

"But Mika—"

"Will have a gargoyle on the inside boosting her. Keeping the *Hopper* stable above the aerie long enough for all of us to escape is going to take all of Patrick's considerable flying skills and more magic than he possesses without your help."

The deck jolted sideways, buffeted by a savage gust. I

stumbled into Oliver, clutching his neck and nose. He planted his wing tips on either side, steadying us as the men poured magic into the levitation spells. The *Happy Hopper* bounced and spun in a slow twist. Ropes groaned and boards creaked alarmingly.

If I survived this, I was never, *ever* flying again.

Marcus trotted to the railing and bent in half over the drop-off. The aerie no longer floated in the distance. It was beneath us, huge and curved and spinning with so much magic that the air around it pressed against my lungs, hindering my breaths. Or maybe my dread was simply so thick it saturated the air.

I watched, numb, as Marcus stripped off his shirt. Not even the sight of his tanned chest, curved with muscles and perfect enough to be cataloged as a work of art, could lessen my terror, but it did unlock my joints. Wobbling, I bent and unlaced my boots. My fingers shook, making the simple task take far too long—and not long enough. My thoughts bolted from one fear to the next, like a hare with a pack of foxes after it. Patrick could lose control of the *Hopper* and crash into the aerie. The people inside could drown. The awanyus could attack. Marcus and I could be pushed from the aerie to our deaths.

However, the probabilities all spiraled down to one certainty: If we did nothing, the gargoyle would die.

I toed off my boots and stepped over to the rope.

6

The sun's heat radiated from the wooden deck, the planks rough under my bare soles. A burst of wind rocked the *Hopper*, tossing the ship like a swing beneath the balloon. My socks, abandoned with my boots, tumbled across the deck and flipped overboard. My sturdy boots didn't budge.

"We're going to need to drop fast," Marcus said to Patrick. "Take us out at an angle and be prepared to dive."

Patrick nodded, his expression tense. Magic darted from him in five different directions, adjusting spells. Keeping us afloat.

"Mika." Marcus was suddenly in front of me. "We're almost in position. Here's what you're going to do." He propelled me two steps closer to the railing. I stumbled on graceless feet, stopping with my thighs inches from the top rail, the drop yawning in front of me. I jerked my gaze to Marcus.

"You need to swim to the front of the trapped ship. Find a pole or beam or railing, and tie this rope to it. This is a taut-line hitch." Marcus demonstrated the knot with the end of the rope lying on the deck. Then he handed it to me and made me tie the knot twice on my own. Bristly hemp fibers bit into my palms, and the thickness of the rope made it unwieldy. "Good. Cinch it as tight as possible. Then swim below deck. When Patrick pulls us out, the water is going to resist. You need to be somewhere you can't get shoved off the ship by accident. Got it?"

I nodded shakily.

"Repeat it back to me."

"Tie the knot, get the gargoyle to safety, swim below deck, hang on."

Marcus's eyes narrowed. I thought he would argue. Instead, he said, "This is an underwater air filter." He built the spell slowly so I could mimic him.

Magic shook in my grip, and I lost the spell twice before I completed it. The earth base was easy, a generic layer of magic I could do in my sleep. The threads of wood tugged throughout it didn't give me much trouble, either. Blending air and fire with them, though, tested my magical abilities. While I practiced the spell, Marcus tied the end of the rope around my waist like a belt, tugging it tight and tying it off with an easy-release knot.

When I finished the air filter, Marcus made me disband it and build it again. Urgency pulsed through me, making me clumsy, but Marcus's patience didn't waver. I finally reconstructed the spell, and he showed me how to affix it over my nose and mouth with touches of earth.

"Take a breath."

I inhaled. Air flowed through the spell slower than I liked.

"You'll get less air once you're underwater, but it will be enough. The key is to breathe deep and evenly. Count it: breathe in for three, out for five."

He waited for me to complete a breathing cycle, counting it out as he instructed, even though it felt as if I was moving in slow motion.

"Good. Keeping this spell intact is your primary focus. Got it?"

I nodded.

Marcus tugged on my hand, his thumb pressing into my amethyst scars a hairsbreadth too hard. "Maintaining your air filter is more important than helping the gargoyle, because if you can't breathe, you're of no use to anyone."

"I got it," I said, fear giving my voice an edge.

Marcus's jaw bunched, and he nodded. "I'll be on the opposite end of the ship. We won't be able to communicate once we're inside. I need you to stick to the plan."

"I will."

I yelped when Marcus gripped my hips and set my feet atop the *Hopper*'s railing. Oliver sprang to my side, rock steady on his hind legs, and fanned his wing around me. I clutched him, eyes squeezed shut, trusting my friend to keep me stable atop the foot-wide board.

"Remember, it's just like jumping into a pond."

Marcus's voice came from beside me. I peeked through slitted eyelids. He stood on the railing on my right, gazing down. Sunlight shimmered on the underside of his jaw and wavered across his cheeks, reflecting off the floating lake. I followed his gaze. A dizzying rush of water, awanyu fins, and magic spun beneath us, tugging at my balance. Fighting vertigo, I focused beyond the aerie's churning surface on the wavering, vaguely rectangular shadow inside. No amount of squinting helped me calculate the trapped ship's depth.

"Are you ready?" Marcus asked, half shouting to be heard above the wind kicking off the aerie.

My legs trembled. The gargoyle's energy signature was

directly below me, and barely stronger than before. I managed a jerky nod.

Marcus brushed a kiss against my temple before pressing his lips to my ear. His deep voice rumbled across my eardrum, the vibrations traveling straight down my spine. "You're Mika Stillwater, Gargoyle Guardian. You can do this."

My shoulders straightened, and I let out a shaky exhale. Marcus gave me a final, fierce smile, then sprinted for the rear of the *Hopper* and the rope waiting for him, taking a second to toss my boots below deck along the way.

"I'll be right here," Oliver said. "I won't let anything happen to you."

A dozen terrifying scenarios leapt to mind, all of them ending with me plummeting to my death.

"I love you so much, Oliver." The spell dampened my voice, making me sound as if I were already underwater. A shiver chased goose bumps up my arms.

"Lower!" Marcus shouted.

The *Hopper* dropped fast, caught, and bounced on the suspension cables. A scream froze in my chest when Marcus lost his balance. He caught himself on his hands and knees, the muscles in his arms flexing to hold himself atop the railing. The dirigible's wings popped and creaked, their prolonged quivering thrumming through the soles of my feet.

"Sorry! I didn't—"

"Lower," Marcus barked, cutting off Patrick's apology. "You've got another ten feet."

The ship dropped again, more controlled this time. Wind buffeted the deck and whipped stinging strands of hair into my face. I should have tied it in a ponytail, but I hadn't been thinking.

"Get ready, Mika," Marcus shouted.

My heart thundered in my chest. The spinning surface of the aerie rose toward us, buffeting the underside of the *Hopper*. Mist whipped around the ship, chilling my bare toes and darkening the canvas of the dirigible's wings. Water stretched in all directions. If I didn't look up, it was almost possible to trick myself into believing we were hovering above a highly agitated but perfectly normal lake—the kind nestled in the ground.

An awanyu burst into the air in the *Hopper*'s shadow. Its slitted pupils locked on me, and I jerked, losing my grip on Oliver's water-slick neck. Oliver cupped me with his wing, pinching my shoulders to hold me steady. Frantically, I wiped my hand on my damp pants and latched on to his neck once more, not taking my eyes from the wyrm.

From a distance, the awanyu could have been mistaken for an enormous eel, but not from this close. Four onyx horns longer than my forearms flared from either side of the awanyu's head, curving backward. The moment it cleared the water, a thick topknot flared behind its eyes, the feathers displaying a black ocellus rimmed in yellow, strikingly similar to the osprey's eye. Air and water elements unfurled from its long dorsal fin, surprisingly uniform. Extending gossamer silver fins from its sides, the awanyu glided through the mist-thick air. Twelve feet of copper scales sailed along the aerie's surface before it dove underwater. Like a needle drawing a string, its magic tightened behind it, forming one thread in the aerie's massive spell.

Another awanyu flashed to the surface, then another, drawing their magic around the levitating lake one leap at a time. I marveled at the coordination necessary to keep such a complex spell cohesive. Did the awanyus operate on instinct or communication? More important, what did they think of humans? Were we nuisances or prey? I was a lot larger than an osprey, but the awanyus weren't tiny. The last looked as if it were as long as the *Hopper* and as thick as Marcus's thigh.

"Mika, we jump in three," Marcus yelled.

My head shot up. Black dots danced in my vision.

"One."

Oliver loosened his grip. I clung tighter, using my free hand to double-check the rope around my waist.

"Two."

Inside my head, the trapped gargoyle's energy pulsed faintly. They needed me. I had to do this.

It's just like jumping into a pond, I thought, hearing the echo of Marcus's confident statement overlaying my less-convincing inner voice.

"Three!"

I bent my knees and dove.

In a breathless double-punch, the awanyus' wild magic slapped my face, then the aerie's freezing water engulfed me, tearing at the air filter. Oliver's boost winked out, and my grip on magic faltered as a weaker boost took its place. The spell clinging to my mouth slipped, threatening to disintegrate. Awanyus whipped through the water, heed-lessly battering me. I swam blind, palms and knees knocking against hard copper-scaled bodies, clothes catching on sharp horns. Fire burned down my thigh, and I kicked away from an awanyu whose horns had caught on my pants. The fabric ripped, freeing us both.

My sense of direction was shot, the momentum of my dive hijacked by the frenzied awanyus. Bubbles frothed the wyrm-clogged water, obscuring all but glimpses of blue—sky or water, I couldn't tell. A twist of air magic hammered my torso. Precious air burst from my lungs, and I tumbled like a broken puppet through the seething serpents.

Lungs burning, I stopped searching for an opening and concentrated on the gargoyle energy signatures in my head. Oliver's energy radiated to my right, bright and healthy. The other gargoyle—

Folding in half, I surged through the thinning awanyu bodies toward the weak pulse of the trapped gargoyle. Black dots flecked my sight, consuming the periphery of my vision. A void of blue opened in front of me, a blocky shape in the middle, but I couldn't make my eyes focus. I needed air. Seizing magic, I yanked hard, pulling only a fifth of what I had held outside the aerie. I stopped kicking, concentrating all my attention on reconstructing the filtration spell. The elements drew through my synapses like taffy, painfully slow. Fire licked up my esophagus. If I didn't take a breath soon, I would pass out.

Instinct overruled panic-laced caution. My first gasp nearly imploded the elemental weave, but precious oxygen filled my airways. I shoved more magic into the spell. Pain stabbed my temples, warning me I was drawing too deep from the elements. My third gasp . . . my fifth gasp . . . My chest expanded, air rushing into my lungs, but I couldn't get a full breath.

Count it out, I thought, remembering Marcus's instructions. I slowed my inhalations from one-second hyperventilating breaths to two-second pants while I hunted for Marcus.

Fractured shafts of sunlight speared the water, illuminating the vast aerie. With its clear blue spherical interior, I felt as if I'd been immersed inside a liquid dumortierite seed crystal—one enlarged to the size of a baetyl and equally as deadly to uninvited guests. An assortment of flotsam and fish circled on the endless current. The outer rim rippled with copper wyrm bodies and an alarming kaleidoscope of pale white-blue sky and green-black ground. The blur of water and magic made it difficult to judge the distance between myself and the far edge and impossible to tell how high above the ground we flew.

High enough. If the aerie fell apart, we would all perish.

Light refracted off a stream of bubbles to my right, the shadow of a rope piercing it in an unnaturally straight line. Marcus treaded water, face upturned to mine. Despite feeling as if it had taken minutes to orient myself, he was only five lengths ahead of me. With the filtration spell cloaking his nose and mouth, I couldn't read his expression, but I could guess at his concern.

Belatedly, I clutched at my waist, a bolt of adrenaline shooting through me. Coarse hemp cut into my hands, and I let out a sharp breath. Marcus's knot had held. My line snaked through the awanyus above me, the loose rope jostled back and forth by the serpents' movements. I gave Marcus an exaggerated thumbs-up and hurried to catch up. The filtration spell tugged against my cheeks with each kick, the force of water against my face threatening to rip the earth anchors from my cheeks and chin.

Get to the gargoyle, I instructed myself, then corrected: *Tie the rope,* then *get to the gargoyle.* The sooner we got the ship out of the aerie, the sooner everyone could breathe normally.

Marcus resumed swimming, easily outpacing me, and I turned my attention to the snared ship. It couldn't have been more different from the *Happy Hopper*. Wingless, balloon-less, and with a deeper, wider cabin, it technically wasn't an airship at all. It was a pleasure cruiser, not made to fly more than a dozen feet above the ground. Listing drunkenly, its string of tinted porthole windows gazed blankly at me from wooden planks inlaid with alabaster and emerald.

Anger simmered in my veins. With its expensive embellishments, the cruiser looked like something a full-spectrum nitwit with too much money would own.

If some entitled jerk had endangered this gargoyle's life on purpose, I would make sure they paid. Dearly.

7

M y arms were beginning to burn when the deck of the trapped ship finally came into view. A knot in my chest eased at the sight of a gap in the front rail. I wouldn't have to perform extra magic to attach my rope.

Veering off course from the gargoyle's guiding beacon, I forced myself to swim toward the front of the ship. The deck lay ravaged, broken spokes and busted boards attesting to missing furniture and snapped-off awnings—and to the violent power of the aerie. If Patrick lost control, the awanyus' magic would pulverize the *Happy Hopper*. It was a wonder this ship was still mostly whole.

I scanned the deck a second time. Aside from a snarl of heavy rope near the center, it appeared empty, though the glowing bundle in my head said otherwise.

The rope shifted, revealing the lumpy shadow of a gargoyle beneath the coils. A narrow onyx canine head lifted to track me, sharp ears flexed high. A slender paw clawed at the slick deck. The ropes flexed, then stiffened, yanking the gargoyle back.

Shock made my next stroke clumsy, and I fought my momentum to get a better look, hoping I was wrong.

Someone had tied the gargoyle to the deck.

Fury tunneled my vision, and I altered course. The ship and its horrid inhabitants could wait. Saving the gargoyle came first. Once untied, the gargoyle could decide for themself if they wanted to stay or drop over the side of the ship and let gravity pull them free of the aerie. Oliver had said the humans wouldn't be able to breathe without the gargoyle's boost, but I wasn't sure I cared. If they had enslaved a gargoyle, perhaps they deserved to die.

A school of miniature awanyus darted past, ten or fifteen black-and-copper-speckled bodies spiraling between me and the gargoyle. Twin air and water elements flared in their wake, chaotic and frighteningly powerful. The water corkscrewed into a whirlpool, swallowing me. I spun head over heels, helpless, the filtration spell nearly ripped from my face and fluttering as it unraveled. Grabbing magic, I slapped the elements back into shape. The spell stabilized, and I gulped down oxygen while clawing at the water to slow my spin. When I shoved my billowing hair out of my face, I found myself twenty feet beyond the rear of the ship, my rope crossed with Marcus's.

I visually traced his taut line to the ship. The end was knotted as Marcus had shown me, the binding reinforced with wood and earth magic. Marcus clung to the rear of the ship, holding himself secure below the deck's surface as the babies' riotous magic tore past above him.

The gargoyle's a prisoner, I wanted to shout when Marcus's eyes found mine, but though the air filter allowed me to breathe, it didn't help sound travel through water. We needed to get clear of the aerie. Then Marcus could bring the full weight of the FPD down on these cretins.

Fuming, I waved off Marcus's pantomimed gesture asking if I needed help and kicked toward the ship. After monitoring my progress for a few strokes, Marcus hauled himself over the railing and swam for the dark opening that led below deck. My opinion of the ship's inhabitants didn't improve when I caught sight of the vessel's name painted across the back: *Forbidden Splendor*. Someone thought a lot of themselves.

Marcus hesitated at the open hatch, his concerned eyes tracking me. I considered attempting to mime instructions for him to tie up anyone he encountered. Let the jerks on this ship experience a taste of their own cruelty. But we didn't have time for underwater charades. Instead, I gave him an exaggerated thumbs-up and kept swimming. After a second, Marcus disappeared into the ship, and I turned my attention to the smattering of infant awanyus zipping within the floating lake. Trails of elemental magic flared behind the young wyrms as they darted from a cluster of twigs and leaves to a school of yellow perch, seeming to take delight in scattering them.

Breathing harshly through the filter, I fought against a current I hadn't noticed when it had been against my back. It wasn't until I was closer to the *Splendor* again that the resistance lessened. I craned my head to look up, then down. The ship drifted dead center in the massive sphere. Without the ability to propel itself past the endlessly circling awanyus and their magic, the ship drifted at the mercy of the swirling of the aerie, trapped at its heart.

Silken alabaster caressed my fingertips as I shoved off the side of the *Splendor*, kicking toward the deck. I crested the railing just as a power-happy pack of baby awanyus careened along the deck. With a strangled gasp, I locked an arm through the railing. The horned wyrms twisted to bounce their magic off the deck's planks, then surfed the blast out into the aerie. The magical shock wave hit my face and arm, tearing at my grip. I closed my eyes, riding out the elemental bombardment like a barnacle.

When I opened my eyes, the front of the ship pointed twenty degrees down. The gargoyle hung sideways in the ropes, their eyes locked on me. Half their body lay hidden in the depression of an iron fire pit sunken into the deck boards, the slick surface giving the gargoyle zero purchase. Ropes bound their wings to their body, then snaked through three silver D rings screwed around the fire pit's perimeter. In a normal situation, those rings probably anchored to a cooking apparatus, but their use had been perverted into a gargoyle snare.

Why would the gargoyle continue to boost the people who had done this to them?

Frustrated, I pulled myself along the railing toward the front of the ship. Getting tossed around by the baby awanyus had wasted precious time. I no longer had a spare moment to free the gargoyle before tying my rope to the *Splendor*, but swimming past the gargoyle felt like a betrayal, especially with their forlorn gaze pressing heavily between my shoulders.

"I'm coming for you," I promised, water garbling my words beyond recognition.

At the tip of the cruiser, I slid my leg through the railing and locked my ankles together. Secured, I tugged at the knot around my waist with cold-clumsy fingers. For a panicked second, I couldn't loosen the knot. Then it sprang free, and I threaded the coarse rope around the thickest beam in the railing, twisting it into the taut-line hitch Marcus had shown me. Grinding my teeth at the delay, I carefully double-checked each loop. Getting the knot right was paramount to our rescue, but my instinct to rush to the gargoyle made each second of the task stretch interminably.

Releasing my leg lock on the railing, I held the end of the knot, planted a foot against the ship, and tugged with all my might. The knot cinched tight. The front of the ship rose, stealing my balance as the *Hopper* rose, drawing the line taut. My relieved exhale clouded my vision with bubbles, and I shoved toward the gargoyle. Earth magic trickled to me, strangled in the awanyus' maelstrom of air and water. I reshaped what I could hold, tuning it to living quartz, adding doses of the other four elements until it sang in harmony with gargoyle anatomy.

My magic reached the gargoyle before I did, sliding gently into their—*his*—body. I grasped the rope confining him seconds later. Pain spiked through the gargoyle with the snap of his bindings, jolting through our connection and straight into my brain. With a muffled cry, I released the rope. Momentum spun me across the deck. Twisting, I half crawled, half swam back. This time, I grabbed a D ring to anchor myself.

The gargoyle's wing was broken. I could see it clearly with my magic, though the injury remained hidden under the rope.

I yanked on the elements. They oozed into me, the current as thin as a spiderweb and weaker than shale. Fire burned inside my skull, chasing blackness through my vision, but additional earth element remained elusive. Even a patch to dampen the gargoyle's pain proved beyond my limited capabilities inside this cursed aerie.

Reluctantly, I turned my attention to the rope, gently untangling the gargoyle. Multiple lines had been knotted together, and it was only after I tugged two free that I could see him clearly. His small form, not much larger than a house cat, fit easily in the fire pit. Ebony chalcedony dominated his canine face and skinny wings, but soft yellow agate rosettes glistened across his sleek marten body. Sunflower-yellow rings tipped his clawed feet where he clung to the lip of the pit. Fatigue radiated from every muscle in the gargoyle's body, a distant ache compared to the sharp agony of his wing. A failing spell wrapped his muzzle, filtering oxygen from the water. I delicately extracted my magic from the gargoyle and studied the fragile breathing spell.

Marcus swam up to me, hand extended—

The tattoo on the back of the man's hand jerked my head up. Shirtless, dark haired, broad chested, and tan, the stranger was Marcus's twin from the corner of my eye. Straight on, he was a poor imitation: narrower through the jaw, with longer hair, a leaner physique, and black bands of a tribal tattoo looping his left side from his knuckles to his shoulder and down one half of his bare chest. A combination of water weight and poor tailoring pulled his pants down to the edge of indecency, exposing a coil of black ink wrapped around his hip.

Planting my left foot in the fire pit with the gargoyle and hooking the toes of my right foot through a D ring, I grabbed a rope floating at my hip. The line no longer coiled around the gargoyle, but it remained tied to a D ring. Suitably anchored, I braced myself between the stranger and the gargoyle. He had to be half a foot taller than me, with an extra forty pounds of muscle, but in the water, with limited magic and him without leverage, I thought I stood a chance of defending the gargoyle from anything he might try.

The man jerked away from me, raising both palms in a pacifying gesture. Gravity pulled him down until his feet rested lightly on the deck. I glanced behind him, searching for Marcus, but he was nowhere in sight. I was on my own.

A quartz paw brushed my bare foot. The gargoyle stared up at me, a plea in his eyes. For me to protect him? Or to free him?

When I glanced up, the man extended a balance of elements to me, silently offering to combine his magic with mine. Linking with a stranger went against my better judgment, especially a stranger who kept gargoyles imprisoned. But more magic would help me reinforce the gargoyle's breathing spell.

Narrowing my eyes, I accepted the man's magic, ready to break the link if he tried anything suspicious. Stifled elements funneled into me, bringing with them the sensation of a nourishing spring on a lazy summer day. For such an imposing figure, the man's magical signature was surprisingly tender. More important, the gargoyle's boost echoed inside his magic. Whatever his relationship to this gargoyle, the marten didn't see him as an enemy. At least not right now. That could easily change once we were beyond the aerie's boundaries.

Black and copper squirmed in the corner of my eye. I hunched as wild elemental magic slammed into my back. My feet flew from the deck, but my grip on the rope held. I thrust a hand toward the stranger. His fingers seized my wrist, the weight of his body wrenching hard on my shoulder joint as the unfocused magic pelted us with the strength of a gale-force wind. My hand slid on the rope, pain igniting across my palm. Shoved from the fire pit, the gargoyle scrabbled stone claws against the slick deck, but he couldn't get purchase. In a rush, he tumbled beneath us and out of reach. Thanks to me, the ropes previously tethering him flapped uselessly. Only one line was still knotted to him, and it unraveled as the awanyus' magic swept the gargoyle toward the *Splendor*'s edge. Terror-wide eyes sought mine. If he fell overboard without a rope tied to him and without the use of a wing, he'd die.

And it would be my fault.

A knot caught, jerking the gargoyle to a halt less than two feet from the edge. His head whipped around, his strong canine jaws locking on the taut line. The stranger and I exhaled at the same time, tandem streams of bubbles spiraling into the void around us.

The infant swarm darted off. The *Splendor* listed to the right, then slowly leveled out. The man released my arm, and we both swam for the gargoyle. The marten's bite had shredded his air filter, and I hastily reformed it, anchoring it securely to his muzzle with twists of quartz-tuned earth. The stranger reached the gargoyle first and scooped his stone body into his arms, cradling the winged marten gently.

The man's concern for the gargoyle and the gargoyle's trust in him punched a big hole through my captive theory. The gargoyle would sink like a stone if he attempted to swim, and he couldn't fly. Tying him to the ship might have been a safety measure—one that wouldn't have been necessary if they had simply taken the gargoyle below.

Confused, I gestured to the gargoyle, then to the shadowy opening of the stairs to the cabins. The man nodded and bent to finish freeing the gargoyle. I tugged magic through our link, amassing enough to stitch a crude elemental bandage over the gargoyle's fractured wing. It lessened the gargoyle's pain, but it wouldn't hold if the gargoyle moved too much.

The rope fell from the gargoyle, but the man didn't start swimming. I gestured again at the opening. He pointed to the rope and the gargoyle's wing, then pantomimed binding his own arm to his side. A sling! I nodded emphatically. The link twanged inside my head, a gentle but insistent tug pulling against it.

I relinquished control to the stranger, silently urging him to hurry. In a flash, he cut the rope with a blade of ice. Pain spiked behind my eyes at the sharp surge of magic. The man winced, too, then surprised me by surrendering the link to my control again. He was stronger, not full-spectrum strong, but definitely more powerful than me. It would have been easy enough for him to keep control.

The ship lurched. My toes crunched into the deck. I windmilled my arms to stay in place, scanning frantically for nearby awanyus. The rope attached to the front of the *Splendor* canted at a forty-five degree angle. I whipped around to check the rear of the ship, shoving aside my cloud of hair. The back line slanted at a matching angle. An electric surge of terror and relief shot through my limbs. Patrick was pulling us out.

I grabbed the man's arm and tugged him toward the stairs. Tucking the quartz marten protectively against his bare chest, the man kicked off the deck. The *Forbidden Splendor* sped beneath us faster than I expected. I overshot the opening and twisted to catch the lip. The man seized the other side and gestured for me to enter first. It took the strength of both my arms to pull myself into the open hatch, working against the drag of water as the *Splendor* cut through the aerie.

Inside the stairwell, the water stilled. I waited for the man and gargoyle to join me, staying near the top of the stairs to use the limited light while we bound the gargoyle's injured wing to his side with the severed rope. I took a second to shore up my elemental bandage, wishing I had thought to stuff a couple seed crystals in my pockets. Not that I could have done much healing here with the little amount of magic I could pull inside the aerie.

The man pointed into the darkness below us, and I nodded. Bending in half, I swam down with one hand on the sloped roof, the other groping in front of me. The stranger followed on my heels. The energy inside my head told me the gargoyle was with him even if I couldn't see the marten's ebony body in the dim light.

We'd made it. We were safe.

A wall of water element punched me from below. I slammed into the stairs, skin scraping carpeted wood. My foot connected with something soft. My head hit something much harder. The link snapped. Dazed, I flailed uselessly as magic shoved me from the stairwell. By sheer luck, I caught the edge of the opening with my fingertips. My arm jerked in its socket, but I managed to hang on as a fountain of water surged from below.

A ribbon of young awanyus speared from the stairwell. Their wild magic ripped at my breathing spell, but I barely noticed. The edge of the aerie loomed beyond the bow of the ship. Adult awanyus churned the curved surface, lambasting the ropes attaching us to the *Happy Hopper*. If I didn't get below deck before the *Splendor* shoved through their frenetic mass, I wasn't sure I would survive. The wyrms were only working to keep their aerie whole, but that wouldn't prevent them from pulverizing me in their frenzy or knocking me from the ship before it cleared the aerie. Or worse: knocking me from the ship *after* it cleared the aerie.

I kicked hard, tightening my grip on the hatch. Dread numbed my body when I spotted the man. He clung to the wrong side of the railing with both hands, muscles straining to pull himself back onto the ship.

I spun, sensing the gargoyle behind me.

The marten clung to the railing, eyes wild with panic. The onslaught of awanyu magic eased, but the *Splendor* picked up momentum, and the countercurrent overpowered the small gargoyle. Desperation flared in his eyes as he shoved from the railing in a wild jump. His solid-quartz weight pulled him to the deck, but his churning legs gained no momentum. My heart lurched in my chest when the current flipped him head over tail and slammed him into the top rail. Only his quick scrambling kept him from being shoved overboard to his death.

I let go.

The current towed me toward the rear of the ship. Hunched, I let it take me, slipping hands and feet along the deck in a futile attempt at control. The top rail slammed into my butt. One foot slipped through the rails. The other caught on a baluster. I grabbed the gargoyle with both hands and brought him to my chest. His slender body was longer than my torso, but not by much. If not for the buoyancy of the water, I wouldn't have been able to lift him. Here, I hoped to use his weight to our advantage.

Tugging my foot free of the railing, I half ran, half swam toward the cabin opening, my body canted at a forty-five-degree angle. The pressure of the current kept the gargoyle plastered to my chest, and I felt his hind claws curl into my waistband. Water assailed me, heavy as molasses, turning my leaps into wretchedly small steps. I hadn't made it halfway back to the opening when three adult awanyus snaked from the stairwell. Magic ripped through the water, exploding outward.

I hugged the gargoyle and dove for the railing. The awanyus' magic bludgeoned my shoulders and hips. I slammed into the railing, forearms crunching between the wooden slats and the gargoyle. Air burst from my lungs in a gush of bubbles. Pinned by waves of awanyu-generated magic, I couldn't adjust the gargoyle. He was secure, but the pressure on his broken wing had to be excruciating. Finally, the weight on my back eased. Through the curtain of my hair, I watched the stranger drag himself over the railing and onto the *Splendor*. His eyes met mine as he wove his arm through the railing to lock himself in place.

Get to the hatch, I mentally urged him.

Heeding my own advice, I braced my feet against the railing and—

The bow of the ship was missing.

Fear broke across my scalp and raced icy tingles down my body. No, not missing. Freed. The first two feet of the *Splendor* hung outside the aerie. The rest of the ship was following fast. My chance of getting into the hatch had passed.

Awanyus circled the *Splendor* in a chaotic fervor, flinging themselves and their magic around the torn edges of the aerie. Wild bands of air and water ripped across the deck as they patched the aerie, even as the *Splendor* ripped a hole through it. In the minuscule gaps between them, I glimpsed the *Happy Hopper*'s dark shape, an indistinct blob surrounded by bright blue. A shimmer of carnelian flashed past, and a blaze of energy moved inside my head with it, tracking Oliver.

Magic punched my knee. My foot slipped, and I floated for one heart-stopping second above the deck, bereft of a handhold. Then the gargoyle's weight tugged us both down. I ducked my head and snaked an arm through the railing, curling protectively around the gargoyle. Scales slid across my back, curved horns gouging my shoulder. The awanyus' magic followed, smashing me to the deck. Wishing I had time to be gentle, I used a knee and fist to flip the gargoyle so his feet were pressed to the railing. He sank quartz claws into the wood, then clamped his jaw around a post.

Muted thunder rumbled through the water, the slap and thump of dozens of awanyus hitting the ship and aerie surface disorientingly distant. We had to be close, though. I wished I had time to tie the gargoyle down again, and myself with him.

A slick body slammed into my side, bouncing me hard against the deck. I grunted and scrambled for a foothold. Magic blasted me from the opposite direction, yanking my legs from the railing. Pain punched my thighs and chest. The mob of wyrms bombarded me. Straining, I reached for the gargoyle, terrified the awanyus would knock him from overboard. Copper shot past my face in a blur, the slap of a tail across my cheek tearing the filter from my mouth. My grip on the railing slipped.

My fingers closed on water.

I twisted and kicked, desperately searching for the gargoyle, the railing, even the deck. I couldn't see past the flurry of copper and frothing water, couldn't find a solid surface among the thrashing wyrms.

Don't let me die here!

Wood bashed my forearm. The railing! Desperation lent me strength, and I punched through the awanyus before they could drag me away, seizing the railing.

Blinding sun hit my face and sound burst against my eardrums, deafening claps and splashes jumbled with indistinct shouts. Air rushed into my starved lungs. An avalanche of magic poured into me from two gargoyles. And gravity grabbed my ankles and yanked.

8

Terror strangled my scream. My feet hung over open air. Lots and lots of open air. My chest scraped against the *outside* of the *Splendor*, my precarious fingerhold on a railing post the only thing keeping me from plunging to my death. Straining, I tried to pull myself up. My biceps quaked. I kicked my legs, searching for a toehold, but the airship's rear wall curved inward, beyond my reach.

Craning my head up, I searched for a better purchase. The tail end of the stone marten dangled above me. The gargoyle clung by a claw to the ship, his one good onyx wing splayed, the other trapped against his body. I shoved a platform of air beneath his hind legs and heaved him onto the deck. Pain exploded in my brain, the magic overload darkening the edges of my vision. My hands slipped on the slick wood. Fire burned through my forearms. I couldn't hold on much longer.

"Mika!" Oliver's shout pierced the air. A carnelian meteor cut through the sky, Oliver's glowing energy inside my head

flipping to the dizzying location *beneath* me. Stone feet braced against my soles, and Oliver flapped hard, lifting me. It wasn't more than an inch or two, but it was enough for me to get a better grip. I sobbed my thanks.

"Hang on. He's coming," Oliver panted, his words choppy as he strove to support me.

A warm hand seized my forearm, and a boost of air magic hit my feet. The tattooed man bent over the railing, his face shadowed by the *Hopper* above us.

"Let's get you aboard," he said.

"Hurry," I pleaded.

Marcus could have lifted me with air alone, but this man was weaker, and it took a combined effort of muscle and magic to hoist me over the railing. The top board scraped my stomach and bruised my knee, but I hardly noticed as I flopped to the deck. My arms possessed the strength of cooked noodles, and my chest heaved as I tried to catch my breath. Afraid I would vomit, I stayed on all fours instead of flopping onto my back. My savior collapsed to his butt beside me and gave me a wan smile. I tried to convey my gratitude with a nod, too winded to speak. The marten loped to my side, pressing against my wet pants. I stroked a trembling finger down his neck and tracked Oliver in my head. My friend coasted around the *Splendor*, staying airborne when I would have preferred to lock him in a hug.

"Marcus?" I croaked.

"Right here."

A knot of tension in my gut unraveled at the sound of Marcus's voice, and I would have collapsed if he hadn't wrapped an arm around me, lifting me to my feet. His body heat seared my chilled flesh when I flung my arms around his waist, pressing my cheek to his bare chest. His heart pounded loud and fast beneath my ear, audible above the creaks and groans of the tethered ships and the raucous bird cries.

The deck quivered, bobbing and rocking out of sync with the *Hopper*. A flurry of wind battered the *Splendor*, driving stinging mist into my face. Behind us and slightly starboard, the torn aerie hemorrhaged water. Awanyus churned around the rift, weaving their magic into their monstrous spell. Foot by foot, the opening closed, cutting off the escaping water.

A splash and gasp jerked my attention to the hatch. Three men knelt on either side of the water-filled opening. One cradled an arm to his chest. Another held a hand against his side, blood leaking from beneath his fingers. The last reached into the water and helped a fourth man flop onto the deck. Exhaustion hung heavily on their bare shoulders, and they darted fearful glances from the *Hopper* to the creaking suspension ropes to the ground disastrously far beneath us.

A message bubble plummeted from the *Hopper* and tore open next to Marcus. Patrick's voice burst out, breathless and strained.

"I can't control our descent. The balloon is barely holding its shape. If I let out any air, it'll collapse, and we'll all be vulture shit by nightfall. If it rips . . ." Muffled curses tumbled from the spell, then Patrick's voice projected loud and clear. "Lose the water weight, or we die."

I stared at the water sloshing in the hatch with numb horror. The *Hopper* wasn't designed to tow another airship, let alone one burdened with a tonnage of water. No wonder Oliver hadn't landed. I braved a glance beyond the railing. Ragged foothills bunched far beneath us, the dense green canopy broken by jagged outcroppings of granite that seemed to draw closer as I stared. Wavering refractions of sunlight glinted across the wet deck, and I twisted to find the aerie. It spun through the air more than ten ship lengths off the left side, already above the *Hopper*. We were sinking. Fast.

Blood rushed from my head, a counterweight to the dizzying lightness shooting up my spine.

"Link up, and tell me your name," Marcus ordered, and all eyes jerked to him. "We'll work faster if we can communicate effectively. I'm Marcus."

Marcus accepted my balance of elements first, and I found a grounding anchor in the familiar sensation of hardened rosewood guarded by a lightning-studded shield of flames. Through Marcus's signature, I could feel Oliver and the smaller gargoyle enhancing Marcus's magic.

"I'm Mika," I said for the other men's benefit. "Can you levitate us to the *Hopper*?"

"We need to halt our free fall first." Marcus balled up earth element as he spoke, punching through the porthole windows down one side of the ship, then the other. He didn't draw on our link, not needing our combined magic for such a simple spell.

Releasing me, he jogged to the railing, leaning far over the edge to peer down the side of the *Splendor*. Cold air swept my side where he had been standing. Goose bumps broke down my skin, and I shivered.

Impatiently, Marcus gestured for the tattooed man to link up. The stranger introduced himself as Nicholas, and his nourishing spring signature slid beneath Marcus's fiery shield.

"Angus," hissed one of the injured men. A bonfire

teetering on the edge of a fireball joined the swirl of magical signatures. With a shaved head, black vine tattoos twining down his ropy forearms, and the same brown eyes, Angus was a lean copy of Nicholas, though much stronger in fire. Wincing, he cradled his arm to his chest as Nicholas helped him stand. Purple bruises radiated from a gash along Angus's bicep, and an angry red slash bisected his bare torso.

Marcus spun together a new, larger spell, drawing magic through the three of us, but I lost track of the pattern when one of the men by the hatch charged toward me.

"I'm Dresden," he shouted, tossing a balance of elements to Marcus. A gust of wind across warm sand joined the link as Dresden dropped to his knees in front of me. I backed up, but Dresden ignored me, bending to embrace the gargoyle.

"Felix, you brave, wonderful gargoyle, are you all right?"

"The guardian saved me," Felix said in a startlingly deep voice.

Dresden tipped his face up to me, revealing a short black beard and mustache and kind, puzzled brown eyes. A silver claw suspended on a leather necklace glinted against his pale chest. "A guardian?"

Now wasn't the time for explanations. Magic siphoned through me as Marcus wove the elements in thick bands, folding and twisting them to repair the *Splendor*'s mangled levitation spells. Our descent didn't noticeably slow, and neither did Marcus. In rapid succession, he built and secured four more levitation spells to the underside of the ship, fluidly incorporating the next man into the link without breaking his concentration.

"Jonathan," the man said, adding a strong dose of wood energy to the link along with his signature of thick birch roots delving into loamy soil. He didn't look away from his wounded companion. Like the rest, Jonathan appeared to have lost his shirt in the aerie. Two bold red-and-black tattoos faced off atop his massive pectoral muscles, a stylized thunderbird on the left, and a mishepishu on the right. Or perhaps it was a pixiu. It was hard to see the creature behind his long brown hair and the injured man leaning against him.

"This is Liran," Jonathan said as Marcus accepted the final man's weak balance into the link.

A silky hot spring wove into the group's magic, thready but strengthening as Marcus steadied the link. A hasty elemental bandage overlaid Liran's ribs, but blood trickled down to stain his low-slung pants. Marcus tweaked the spell, and Liran gasped, then straightened with a tight-lipped nod of thanks. The ooze of blood slowed.

I was the only person on deck wearing a shirt. I was also the only person who didn't look like I could cart around a small gargoyle or two under each arm.

What sort of ship was this? *Forbidden Splendor* wasn't the sort of name an elite family would typically choose for their leisure craft. These men weren't full spectrums, either. I could feel as much through the link. They had their individual strengths, but none of them came close to matching Marcus's power. They were fit but lacked any telltale calluses to denote a trade. More important, they had Felix as a companion. And from what I could tell, the gargoyle seemed to genuinely want to be with them.

"The water's not draining fast enough," Nicholas said, peering over the side.

"Agreed," Marcus said.

"We don't need the whole ship," Dresden said. "Just the deck. Cut the rest—"

"If I do that, the deck will fold in on itself." Marcus demonstrated with a clap of his hands. I wasn't the only person to jump.

"Where is the hull the most reinforced?" he asked.

"The rear?" Angus suggested.

Nicholas nodded. "Aft starboard. This far from the bottom." He held his arms two feet apart.

A blade of fire and earth dove over the back rail. Through the link, I felt it puncture the lacquered boards. Water spurted through the narrow opening, and Marcus poured more fire element into his simple spell before it could be doused.

A cacophony of pops and creaks ran through the rear of the ship. The deck quivered. Marcus sprinted to the back and bent over the railing, Nicholas beside him.

"It's tearing up the ship," Nicholas exclaimed, his voice all but lost beneath the rising racket.

Magic burst from Marcus, patching the puncture. The ship continued to crack, fragile seams threatening to split. If even one board broke, the water pressure would rip the rest apart, taking the deck with it.

Marcus pelted the ship with earth and wood magic, damming gaps and strengthening the ship's frame—and preventing any more water from escaping to lighten the *Splendor*.

"What now?" Angus asked.

"Barely anything is draining out the portholes," Jonathan said, his words faint as he leaned over the side railing. "That's half the ship's water weight. Maybe it was enough?"

I checked the horizon. Our descent hadn't slowed.

A shriek eerily close to a harpy's jerked everyone's head up. Splinters rained from the ship-long fracture that snaked across the bottom of the *Hopper*. I ducked my head beneath my arm to protect my eyes, then stumbled to one knee when the *Splendor* convulsed. The vibration raced back up the tow lines, and the rift in the *Hopper* widened with a tortured squeal. Oliver dropped through the air seconds ahead of a message spell.

"Patrick needs help!" he shouted.

Marcus wrapped a wood-and-earth patch across the *Hopper*'s growing fracture, simultaneously catching the message and activating it. Patrick's panic-laced voice spilled out.

"I've reinforced the ship with everything I've got. The ropes are fraying. The balloon is V-ing. We've got two minutes, tops. Maybe only one."

Marcus's eyes met mine, and my heart sank. Even with the power of our combined magic, Marcus couldn't lift everyone to the *Hopper* at once. Levitating us one at a time or in pairs would take too long.

"I can get you up there," Marcus said, his gaze burning into mine.

I shook my head. I wouldn't abandon him. "There has to be another way."

"More levitation spells?" Liran suggested.

"Won't work," Marcus said.

"No room," Nicholas added, having been part of the link when Marcus built the spells lining the bottom of the ship.

"And the ship's too fragile," Marcus said. "Any additional upward pressure will punch through the bottom."

I peeked at the approaching horizon, then jerked my gaze back to Marcus. A ridiculous, terrifying idea swam through my thoughts, the kind of crazy-brave scheme I would have expected from Marcus. I was scared to even voice it, but we were running out of time.

"We've already got one big hole in the ship," I said. If the wind whipping across the deck had been any louder, it would have drowned out my voice. My finger shook as I pointed to the hatch. The opening leading down to the cabins was at least five feet wide. It just happened to be on the wrong side of the *Splendor*. Through numb lips, I forced out the rest of my poorly hatched plan. "Can we roll the ship?"

Marcus's eyebrows shot to his hairline. "That . . . could work."

"And we'll do what?" Jonathan asked. "Hang on?" His eyes flicked to Angus, who clutched his injured arm to his chest.

"I can manage," Angus said, convincing no one.

"We'll have to climb along the ship to stay on the top side," I said, trying to sound confident. Once the ship was flipped and the water drained, the *Hopper* could support us long enough to get us safely to the ground.

"Any additional torque on the ropes is going to rip that ship apart," Nicholas said, his eyes on the *Hopper*.

As if it agreed, the *Hopper* shrieked, another long rip opening down the length of its hull.

"I'll make sure we give it slack. Everyone, to the railing!" Marcus yelled. "Jonathan, Dresden, assist Liran. Nicholas, you've got Angus. Felix, Mika, to me."

I sprinted to Marcus's side, gripping the railing with both fists. Felix squeezed himself on my left, between me and Marcus. The men arranged themselves along the railing to my right. Nicholas's worried eyes met mine, then dropped to Felix. The gargoyle curled a cool paw around my toes, leaning his small body into my shin. Trust radiated from his canine eyes, and I realized he wasn't clinging to me for reassurance; he was offering it.

I took a deep breath, firming my resolve to live up to the faith Felix—and Oliver, and every gargoyle who saw me as a guardian—placed in me.

When I looked up, Nicholas gave me a nod and turned his attention to Angus. I studied the line of men. Exhaustion pinched their features, but each stood braced, one hand on the railing, their arm muscles tense and their knees bent. Even Liran managed to appear ready for this insane stunt, despite the jagged cut along his ribs. Whoever these men were, they weren't cowards, and they weren't lazy, high-society fops. If we survived, I looked forward to learning how they had earned Felix's loyalty.

"Can you toss Felix up to the *Hopper*?" I asked Marcus, wanting at least one of us to be safe.

"I'm sorry, but I'll need his boost."

I frowned. The *Hopper* was more than close enough to keep the gargoyle's boost in range.

I flinched in unison with the men when Marcus yanked more magic through us, building a massive spell. He formed a second spell at the same time, this one a simplistic sound-capturing configuration, and spoke into it. I couldn't hear his voice, but I read his lips.

"Dive."

Marcus tuned the message to Oliver and released it. The bundle of elements speared skyward to where the energy in my head told me Oliver soared on the opposite side of the *Hopper*. Marcus sent a second message to Patrick, but the implications of his first message seared panic through my thoughts, and I missed what he said. The second message blasted away.

"Everyone, *hang on*," Marcus bellowed, nearly deafening me. Grabbing Felix, he tucked the small gargoyle against his side.

Oh merciful gods.

I locked an arm around the railing. In synchronized slashes of fire, Marcus cut the ropes tethering us to the *Hopper*.

The *Splendor* dropped out from beneath me.

9

M y feet went weightless. Raw terror exploded through my body. I screamed, the sound lost to the ether as we fell. The horizon jumped and began to climb. My arms jolted around the railing, slamming me back to the deck, jarring my vision and snapping my teeth together. Wind whistled past my ears, yanking my wet hair into a snarl above my head. The deck tipped, the opposite side canting away from me. My bare toes slid on wet planks. I tightened my grip on the railing, my thoughts an incoherent stream of prayers. Magic tore through my brain, funneling into a massive spell I couldn't comprehend in my panicked state.

"Climb over!" Marcus yelled.

He threw a leg over the railing, letting it dangle over open air. The men mimicked him, straddling the top rail. I stared at the forest racing closer. Once artificially flattened by distance, the landscape now rolled and jutted in visible hills. Sharp, hard, deadly hills. Hills covered with brutal trees, jagged rocks, and crushingly hard surfaces.

I trembled, mesmerized by the speed of the approaching

treetops. My toes curled into a deck slowly tipping away from me, my eyes locked on the side of the ship rising to fill my view.

"Mika! Now!"

I jerked, breaking my trance. The deck slid from beneath my feet. I squeaked and scrambled to throw a leg over the railing. Marcus clutched my waistband, hauling me fully atop the railing. I teetered on the thin plane of wood, both my legs dangling over slanted surfaces that would do nothing to prevent my fall if I slipped. Then Marcus's enormous spell tipped the ship past the halfway point, and the side of the *Splendor* began to level.

"Get ready to run," Marcus shouted. He pulled his dangling leg up, rising to a coiled crouch.

I curled both legs beneath me. The railing dug into my knees and palms. The thought of letting go made me want to cry. Why had I come up with this idiotic plan?

I locked eyes with Felix, who was tucked tight against Marcus's side. The small gargoyle held perfectly still, his expression a gut-wrenching mix of fear and faith. I readied a blade of earth but left the simple spell unformed. If this failed, I would cut the rope securing his injured wing to his side and shove him from Marcus's grip into the air before we crashed. With a wing and a half and Oliver's help, Felix would have a chance of surviving.

A shuddering groan ran through the ship, shaking the boards beneath me. Water sloshed out the hatch. Wind curled mist from the crest of the wave, and I tipped my chin to avoid the worst of the stinging droplets. The deck popped and groaned again. Another sloshed wave escaped, then a waterfall spilled from the *Splendor*.

"*Move!*" Marcus bellowed.

The ship's rotation sped up, tipping my precarious perch

toward the ground as the ponderous exodus of water flipped the ship faster than Marcus's spell. I lurched to my feet, bracing the sole of my right foot on the underside of the railing. Marcus maintained a steely fist around my waistband, Felix clutched in his opposite arm. Together, we dashed up the tilting ship. The boards vibrated underfoot, the slap of bare feet against wet wood filling the air as Jonathan, Nicholas, Dresden, Liran, and Angus ran with us.

Fifteen feet of gently bowed planks stretched between us and the bottom of the ship—soon to be the top of the ship. I kept my gaze locked on the rising base of the *Splendor*, refusing to think about the deadly drop looming behind me, refusing to acknowledge the lack of safety spells to catch us if we slipped.

I failed to notice the row of slick alabaster shells and emerald inlay until it was too late. My foot landed on a polished shell and slid out from under me, and I crashed onto my hip. Marcus's grip was torn from my pants. Immediately, I scrambled to all fours, digging for purchase with my fingers and toes as I continued to slide. The emptiness behind me pulled like a physical force, eager to plunge me to my doom.

Marcus lunged to catch me, but I was already out of reach. Peeling a tendril of magic from the myriad spells he juggled, Marcus thrust solid air beneath my heels. I jerked to a halt. A rush of euphoria swept up my back like sandpaper. Air rasped in my lungs, a matching fire to the pain of my torn fingernails. I longed to drop flat and hug the ship, but if I didn't get moving, I would be dumped off the side.

Tentatively, I took a step, keeping three other points of contact with the lacquered hull. Marcus's elemental foothold dissipated, dissolving into the maelstrom of magic he kept in motion around the *Splendor*. When I didn't slip, I chanced another step. Jonathan and Dresden powered past Marcus with Liran supported between them. The injured man's feet never touched down. When they reached the beam connecting the side of the ship to the base, they sat, splitting their legs over the two planes of the ship for balance. Nicholas and Angus lagged behind them, and Jonathan had to grab Angus's injured arm to support him when both men half fell into their seated positions.

"Mika, you have to run," Marcus said, his voice eerily calm.

He wove another gargantuan spell, tugging magic through me. I gasped as fire ghosted through my synapses and receded. He was building full-spectrum-level spells on top of each other, each faster than the last. I couldn't decipher one from the next. Anyone else wouldn't have been able to keep them straight. Even Marcus showed strain, his expression flat with concentration, his eyes glassy as he stared at the air between us.

"You too," I panted.

Afraid he wouldn't move until I caught up to him, I shoved into a sprint. My feet slipped and slid, but I stayed upright. Green flashed in my periphery, far too close, and fear tingled up my spine, pressing needles into my chilled flesh. We were running out of empty air. Any minute, we would hit the ground. The inevitability swelled in my mind, consuming my thoughts until only one remained.

Run.

A hop took me over the perilous shells, but each step made less progress than the last as the slick boards grew increasingly steep. Felix moved. I didn't chance a glance up; I felt him shift inside my head, and I sobbed with relief that he and Marcus had made it to the top. The men called to me, urging me to go faster. In a distant part of my mind, spells stacked and folded together, but none of them slowed the ship's roll.

My feet slipped. I caught myself on all fours, but a cry of despair tore from my throat when all my progress slid by, and I stopped barely above the alabaster-and-emerald line.

I looked up. The side of the ship was almost vertical. Only the upward force of the wind and the subtle curve of the hull held me to the surface. Marcus kneeled on all fours, body bowed in agony as he strained to layer spells faster than our free fall. Fire blazed in his eyes when his gaze landed on me.

"Jump." The wind stole the sound from Marcus's shout, but I read his lips.

Jonathan and Nicholas hung over the edge of the ship, arms outstretched for me. The distance between us might as well have been a mile. Even if I had a horizontal foothold to push off from, I wouldn't be able to reach them. But it wasn't the strangers who would catch me. It was Marcus, and I trusted him with my life.

I closed my eyes and leaped.

A golden beacon of energy plunged to meet me. Cool carnelian dragon paws seized my extended arms. I lurched in Oliver's grip. My eyes snapped open, and I locked my hands around Oliver's forearms. Briefly suspended, I had time to take in the astonished expression rounding Dresden's eyes and mouth, to measure the feet between Jonathan's extended fingers and myself—a distance I hadn't come close to closing—to notice the rivulets of water streaming up the side of the ship and the fractures that ran through the beams. Time to take in Marcus's blazing smile, the pride in his eyes lighting a small sun in my chest.

Then we dropped. I clutched Oliver's slick legs, holding my breath. Head thrust back, Oliver pumped the air, slowing us. His huge stone wings beat around me, blinding me to everything but my love for this incredible, brave gargoyle. He couldn't support me indefinitely, but he bought me precious seconds.

The *Splendor* fell. Marcus flashed past, eyes slitted with concentration. I swung my legs over the inverted ship. Three sets of hands grabbed me, and I released Oliver. My toes barely touched the deck before we all sprawled in a heap as the *Splendor* heaved upward to meet me. I landed hard on my hip, my spine grinding against a rigid forearm under my back. The pain registered distantly as I tracked Oliver.

Free of my dead weight, he shot into the sky, then reversed in a fluid dive, spearing back toward me. The ship convulsed. My rasping breath hitched when the *Splendor* tipped. Alarm flared in Oliver's eyes, and he jerked aside. The *Splendor* was yanked in the opposite direction. The top of a tree flashed past, a blur of green. Something heavy hit the underside of the ship, spinning us. I tumbled against Nicholas, clutching at his thigh to stop my roll.

"Hang on," Marcus barked. His jaw flexed, his chest flushed red and the veins in his neck rigid as he strove to keep the ship airborne. We had jettisoned the water that had threatened to split the ship apart, but our descent was still too fast. The new levitation spells Marcus anchored to the deck below us strained to counter the weight and momentum of the ship. If we had more time, another thousand feet to fall, it might have been enough.

The ship rocked to the right. Branches snapped against the underside of the *Splendor*. We bounced. I clenched my teeth as my body lifted then crashed back to the wooden planks. Phantom needles speared my temple as Marcus pulsed magic through a battery of propulsion spells affixed to the sides of the bloated cruiser. The *Splendor* had never

been designed to fly upside down, and its inverted aero-
dynamics worked against us. Only Marcus's quick spell
work kept us from spinning out of control.

Behind us, treetops frothed and snapped. Wind slapped
stinging strands of wet hair against my neck and cheeks.
Pushing myself to my hands and knees, I blinked tears from
my eyes. Liran, Angus, and Jonathan lay sprawled between
me and Marcus. Angus clung to Felix with his uninjured
arm, and Jonathan anchored Liran to the ship. Marcus
punched power through one side of the ship's levitation
spells, and we tipped. I clutched Nicholas tighter as the treetops fell away, the hill beneath them diving into a deep
canyon. Pain lanced my skull as Marcus wrestled the ship
flat, fighting to keep us in line with the snaking gap, pushing
hard against the levitation spells to slow our reckless
descent.

"Dres, get to the side," Nicholas shouted. "Mika, forward.
Go to the center. Distribute your weight."

Dresden scrambled away from us, keeping low, and
braced himself against a beam on the opposite side of the
ship. Nicholas flattened himself in place. Marcus's frantic
juggling of levitation spells slowed. Reluctantly, I peeled my
fingers from Nicholas and crawled toward the center of the
ship. If we survived, I owed him an apology for the bruises
I'd inflicted.

"—do it. Stay with me, Lir—"

Alarm jolted down my spine at Jonathan's fractured
demands. I whipped around to check on Liran. The injured
man stared at nothing, his eyes bloodshot, his jaw locked in
pain. If he fainted, his tie to our linked magic would dissipate. Marcus was barely holding us together as it was. One
fewer person in the link would be catastrophic.

The ship swerved, knocking my arm out from beneath

me. My shoulder and cheek hit the deck hard, and the ringing between my ears temporarily displaced the roar of the wind. I scrambled back to all fours and faced forward.

The ground rushed at us, tall trees like javelins ready to skewer us, rocks eager to pulverize what remained. A strangled scream climbed up my throat. I dug my fingernails into the lacquered planks and hunched lower.

Oliver dove from the left and behind us, sweeping closer.

"Right at the fork," he yelled. He shot past the ship and spread his wings to slow himself, his words half lost to the winds. "... Meadow ... Second bend ..."

I twisted to verify Marcus had caught his instructions. Fiery blue eyes bore into mine, raw with determination and pain. Then magic tore through me, tunneling my vision. The rear of the ship slid to the side. We shot down the right fork of the canyon. Branches battered the underside of the *Splendor*, and a dull crack resonated through the ship, felt more than heard above the howl of the wind.

We plummeted below the treetops, dropping into a channel between two walls of dense trees. Ahead and below us, a river rushed low over a bed of boulders. If we landed at this speed, the ship would be torn apart, and us with it.

Disbanding the spells he had been using to steer us, Marcus reached out with fresh magic into the ground beneath the river, building cushions of air one after the next and locking them into the rock below the soil. We hit the first and obliterated it without slowing. The second and third air cushions sent minor quakes through the ship. The *Splendor* struck the fourth and fifth simultaneously, jolting the entire ship. I flew forward, scrambling to halt myself. My fingertips crunched against a thin crossbeam, and I seized the negligible handhold. A backlash of magic raked jagged spikes through my brain as we crashed through the next series of air cushions faster than Marcus could anchor them, the broken magic imploding inside the link. A huge fallen tree canted across the river, and Marcus shoved a wave of air against the *Splendor*, heaving us around the obstacle with sheer elemental strength. Then the meadow burst into sight, bright yellow in the sunlight and speckled with low bushes and rock outcroppings.

Marcus lined the *Splendor* up with the meadow and . . .

Time slowed as Marcus's control faltered. He slumped over his bent knee, both fists braced against the ship, his head hanging low. Sweat plastered his hair to his scalp and glistened across his bare back. Granite dropped into the pit of my stomach when his next air spell unraveled before it could fully form.

His head lifted, and his eyes met mine. He gathered himself for another spell, his weariness causing the link to waver. Fire licked inside my brain, an echo of the agony radiating from Marcus. One more spell, and he would burn himself out.

I seized control of the link, stealing it from Marcus as easily as if I'd plucked it from a child.

A tsunami of elements swamped me. Unable to parse myself from the others, I drowned in the combined power, lost. A single glowing beacon separated itself from the deluge. I grabbed for it like a lifeline, recognizing Oliver's boost. Familiar, stable, *gargoyle*, it anchored me. Felix's boost gave me another point of control. The echo of both gargoyles' enhancement in all six men pulled me to the surface of the link.

I opened my eyes on a gasping inhale. Rocky soil studded with spiked weeds filled my vision, less than twenty feet from the nose of the airship and approaching faster than a steam engine. Behind me, the men's yells surged to new heights.

I didn't have Marcus's training or spell knowledge. All I had was raw power—more power than I had ever held outside a baetyl—and a burning desire to survive.

I dove the elements into the earth, searching . . . searching . . .

There.

Quartz veined the rocks beneath the soil, close but buried. I twisted the colossal bands of magic in my grasp, tuning it all to quartz and sinking it into the rock. The magic had no finesse. Compared to the complexity of matching a living-quartz gargoyle, it was downright crude. I shoved more power into it, treating the raw mineral like a seed crystal, and *pulled*.

The ground in front of us exploded in a spray of dirt and weeds, a spiral of white quartz spearing from the earth. I shoved the surface of the rock, molding it into something vaguely flat. The *Splendor* crashed the last few feet to the earth, and I yanked the quartz up to meet it.

Wood screeched and crumbled. With a quick flip of magic, I pushed the quartz into the ground, spreading it in front of us like spilled water, redirecting the *Splendor*'s momentum forward instead of shattering the ship against the earth. Pain tore through my brain, then dissipated as I dragged more power from the link. An avalanche of sound consumed me as the levitation spells anchored to the bottom of the *Splendor* ripped free with a hunk of the deck. The ship jerked from my grip, and I flailed blindly for purchase, my eyes locked on the earth in front of me, my senses tuned to the ground beneath the ship.

Steely fingers caged my ankle, slamming me to the ship. I braced my hands beneath me and glanced down. The tip of the *Splendor* sheered away inches from my knuckles. Another foot, and I would have been tossed off the ship—and then flattened beneath it when it ran me over. A distant part of me gibbered in terror, but I didn't have time to indulge it. Dirt pelted me, obscuring my vision as I forced more quartz to the surface. The ship bucked and juddered, the interior shredding layer by deafening layer. An inferno roasted the inside of my skull, overtaxed magic pathways screaming in agony, but I couldn't stop. I needed more power. Tunneling through the link, I reached past the men to the gargoyles boosting their magic. Oliver and Felix were there six times over, their enhancement echoing within the men's magic as if I were boosted by twelve additional gargoyles.

With a primal scream, I redoubled my crude spell, building the quartz into a steep ramp, slowing the *Splendor*. Saplings parted, falling away to either side. The quartz climbed in front of us, forcing the nose of the ship higher, until blue sky and the tops of towering pines were all I could see.

The wind in my face abated. The blur of scenery rushing by slowed. With squeals and cracks, the *Splendor* ground to a halt. Then it began to slide backward, down the quartz slope. It didn't take much effort to curl the lip of the quartz ramp over the front of the *Splendor*, cinching the remains of the ruined ship in a vise of rock.

We halted. My body hummed, my nerves certain we were still in motion. Power crackled through my brain. Panting, I rested my face against the quartz overlapping the wood in front of me, smoothing the jagged edges from it until it felt like a seed crystal beneath my cheek. The gargoyles drew closer, surrounding me.

"—ka. Look at me. Mika."

Marcus sounded as if he were on the far side of a cavern or the wrong side of a mountain. I blinked blearily at the quartz in front of me, trying to make sense of it. It wasn't pure crystalline in structure. It wasn't thrumming with the energy of a gargoyle . . . like it should? For a second, I saw the interior of the baetyl surrounding me, the gigantic bisecting crystals arching over me, the colorful quartz coating every surface. An echo of the baetyl's power swelled in me, and I chased the memory, frustrated when it remained a hairsbreadth out of reach.

"Mika. Let go. You need to release it. Mika, look at me." Marcus gently rolled me over. "Mika, can you hear me?"

"Whoa, look at her pupils," someone said. Dresden, I thought. I had eyes only for Marcus.

He knelt over me, exhaustion adding haggard lines to his concerned expression. I stared into his beautiful blue eyes, and the memory of the baetyl faded. Pain replaced it, eating through my head.

"Are we alive?" I croaked.

"Yes. You did it. We all made it. You can let go. Let the link dissolve."

I frowned uncomprehendingly. The gargoyles were boosting me. I needed to keep the magic together to hold them . . . No, that was an old thought. A baetyl thought.

A moment of disoriented panic swirled through me as I disbanded the link and twelve of the fourteen gargoyles winked out. I checked the beacons in my head, reassuring myself Oliver was close and Felix closer.

A chorus of relieved exclamations echoed among the men. Marcus sighed and collapsed to his back next to me. I raised my head to check on the others, but a fresh wave of pain flattened me.

"Don't try to move yet. You need to—" Marcus interrupted himself with a yawn. "You need to rest."

I closed my eyes. Marcus threaded his fingers through mine, his grip warm and stable. The men began to talk, but their words washed over me. They needed help and healing. So did Felix.

A glowing bundle of energy coasted to the deck, and I reached a feeble hand out to stroke Oliver's chest without opening my eyes. The battered boards creaked beneath his weight, but it was all right. If we fell through, he would catch me.

10

C ool velvet brushed my mind, the caress
waking me.
  Oliver.

A bundle of glowing energy in my head sat so close I
knew before I twitched my fingers that I would find my
friend pressed to my side.

"Marcus?" I croaked.

"He's safe," Oliver said.

"Did he—?" Stringing words together proved too hard. I
needed to see Marcus for myself, but my eyelids remained
glued shut. Blunt fingers dug into my scalp when I tried to
turn my head, holding me still.

"Shh, relax," a stranger said.

Panic pulsed through me, then receded as delicate
elemental ribbons in my head swelled to thick cotton, swad-
dling my thoughts in darkness.

Pain woke me the second time, a sharp stinging radiating from the sole of my left foot. I jerked away from the
source only to be pulled up short by a warm hand circling

my ankle. A rush of sensation tugged through me, and I lunged for a handhold, a scream climbing my throat. I was falling . . .

"I'm here, Mika," Oliver crooned.

My eyes snapped open. My friend crouched beside me, one wing locked over my stomach, his anxious face inches from my nose. Light danced across one side of Oliver, setting his brilliant crimson body aglow against an indigo sky. Blood thrummed in my ears. I twisted, locking a hand around Oliver's leg to anchor myself. I needed to hold on so I didn't . . . so I didn't . . .

Dirt shifted beneath me. Memory of our harrowing landing burst through me, and I lurched upright. Oliver jerked aside, then placed a soothing paw on my thigh. I dropped my hand on top of it, steadying myself. The stranger holding my foot lifted his hands in a pacifying gesture I barely noticed.

"Easy, Mika. We're—"

"Marcus." His name burst from me, relief turning the exclamation breathless. I spun toward his voice, the sudden movement spiking pain through my temples. Marcus sat behind me, where he had been supporting my head while I slept. Firelight softened his smile and played off his muscular chest as he scooted close to wrap an arm around me, holding me as if I were made of porcelain. I leaned into his embrace, savoring his warmth, his existence.

"How do you feel?" he asked.

"Incredibly lucky." I tipped my head up to see his face. "And you? You're not . . . You can still—?"

"I'm not burned out, thanks to you."

Tears stung my eyes, blurring Marcus's tender smile. He had come too close to losing his magic. To losing his life.

Latent fear shivered down my spine, sending a tremor through my limbs.

"Hey, none of that. We made it." Marcus tugged me back against him. I breathed in the clean scent of him as he stroked my hair, focusing on the rise and fall of his chest until the knot in my throat disappeared. Oliver shifted to rest his muzzle against my bicep, encasing us both in a stone-winged hug.

Eventually, I remembered we weren't alone, and I sat up. Marcus kept a hand on my back, the warmth from his palm sinking through the thin material of my top. Oliver bunched himself up on all fours next to me, his tail curled around my hips and his wings trailing behind him. Seated, we were the same height, and I tipped my head to rest my temple against his as I took in my fellow survivors. Angus sat with his arm in a sling next to Jonathan, both of them slumped against a piece of driftwood on the opposite side of the fire. Next to them, Patrick gestured animatedly as he chatted with Dresden and Nicholas, his eye-watering striped shirt blazing bright in the firelight. Liran lay unconscious or asleep on a stretcher of air between the men, with Felix curled tight to his side. The gargoyle's canine eyes glowed as he tracked me, but he didn't lift his head, and his broken wing was still bound in a rope sling.

I tapped the elements, testing my strength. Dull pain throbbed through my skull as I folded together a basic quartz blend, but it could have been much worse.

"Careful," Marcus said.

I nodded, letting him know I heard him, then slid my magic into Oliver.

"I'm tired, nothing more," Oliver said.

My magic confirmed it. Minute fractures speckled his

wing muscles, but I expected nothing less after his break-neck flight, not to mention supporting my weight—twice. His body would mend on its own, but I could speed his recovery.

Oliver shook his head when I gathered more elements. "Save your strength for Felix," he said.

"Velasquez, would now be a good time?" a woman called from the right.

"One moment," Marcus said.

I let my magic dissolve and peered into the deepening gloom. A trio of people stood near the center of the meadow, bodies bowed as they studied the shadowed ground. I didn't recognize any of them, though they wore familiar Federal Pentagon Defense uniforms. The man at my feet was also FPD, his uniform adorned with the leaf symbol of a wood elemental. Marcus introduced him as Calidore, adding, "His squad spotted our landing and rushed to help. You're in good hands."

Our landing. Only Marcus could make a death-defying crash sound so benign.

"I'll be right back." Marcus straightened with a half-swallowed groan and circled the fire, his steps slower than normal.

"He's fine," Calidore said, smiling at me when I focused on him. "I did a bit of patch work on him, but Velasquez is tough. A bit more sleep, and he'll be back to normal."

"You're certain?"

"Positive." Dark curls fell around the healer's face when he bent over my foot again, but the thumb-size glowball he maintained near my toes illuminated his features. "Same with you, once I get the rest of these splinters out." A stab of pain spiked across my sole, soothed in the next breath by a brush of water element. "Five down, a dozen more to go."

"Splinters?" I checked my palms, finding newly mended flesh. A sickly yellow bruise marred my forearm, and a pink line ran down my thigh, visible through the rip in my pants where an awanyu horn had gouged my muscle. Calidore had been busy while I was unconscious. "Splinters can wait," I said. "Felix needs—"

Nicholas dropped to a cross-legged seat in Marcus's abandoned spot, startling me. Dresden sat next to him, crowding Calidore. Jonathan knelt on my other side, one hand lightly petting Oliver as he peered anxiously into my eyes.

"How do you feel?"

"Are you in pain?"

"Are you warm enough?"

Their questions fell on top of each other, leaving no space between them for answers. I blinked at their concerned faces, doing my best not to let my gaze wander lower. Without the fear of falling to our deaths numbing my brain, I was acutely conscious of their half-naked states— especially with the men all but draped over me, the caress of golden firelight across each man's tantalizing torso providing an unexpected level of intimacy.

"Let her breathe," Calidore said, swatting at the men.

Nicholas shifted an inch so his bare shoulder no longer brushed mine. Dresden sidled closer to Nicholas, giving the healer more room, if not me. Jonathan sat, spreading his legs to either side of Oliver and peering over Oliver's shoulder at me. The eye of the thunderbird tattoo on his pectoral muscle peeked over Oliver's shoulder at me, too.

"I'm fine," I said after a pregnant silence reminded me the men were waiting for my response. "That's what—" I winced when Calidore plucked another sliver from my foot.

"You're warm enough? I can add a bit more fire to the spell," Angus offered.

I blinked past Calidore's shoulder at Angus. He hadn't stampeded to my side with the other men, but he *had* shifted closer. Patrick had as well, and their gazes were as rapt as Nicholas's, Jonathan's, and Dresden's. I rolled dirt between my fingertips, unsure where to look, and wished uncharitably that more of them were unconscious like Liran.

"It's cozy," I said, referring to the warming spell that wrapped my body. I hadn't noticed it until Angus pointed it out, but now I realized it had his bonfire signature coiling through the simple elemental pattern. "Perfect," I added, wishing it had been Marcus who crafted the spell instead.

"We owe you our lives," Nicholas said.

The others chorused in agreement.

Flustered, I shook my head. "Marcus was the one who did all the hard work. He knew what to do when we spotted you in the aerie, and he kept us from crashing."

"You were the one who landed us safely," Jonathan said.

I scrunched my face, not wanting to think about that terrifying moment. Oliver patted my thigh comfortingly, his own eyes half closed as Jonathan stroked his scaled throat.

"Velasquez is FPD," Dresden said, then hesitated. "But... ah, you're not, right? It didn't feel like you were, then you did that thing." He held his hands out, palms up, then swept them together and interlaced his fingers.

I frowned at his hands, not sure what he was miming. "I guarantee I'm not a full spectrum. I'm simply a gargoyle healer." My gaze went to Felix again, and I flexed my free foot, wincing as pain flared across the sole.

"She's a gargoyle guardian," Oliver said.

Calidore paused to peer at me. I could feel the other men's curious gazes sharpen on me like pinpricks.

"What's a gargoyle guardian?" Nicholas asked.

"Someone with a special affinity for gargoyles and healing them," I said, hoping to deflect questions I couldn't answer. I braced my hands beside my hips and flexed my arms, testing my physical strength. If I had a bit more room to maneuver or a helping hand, I could stand.

"Is that why you have quartz tattoos?" Dresden asked. His smooth fingertip brushed the back of my hand, sliding over the amethyst hexagons dotting my flesh.

"Not tattoos," I said. "Scars." I curled my fingers toward my palms, fighting the urge to hide my hands. It was too late; they had already seen my scars. Besides, I didn't like the idea of hiding them. I wasn't ashamed of them. They were beautiful, if difficult to explain.

"Any chance you can scar me like that?" Jonathan asked. He leaned away from Oliver and puffed up his chest, gesturing to the thunderbird and mishepishu tattoos on his rounded pectoral muscles. A flex sent one bouncing, then the other. "Don't you think each would look better with a carnelian eye?"

"Put those things away," Nicholas said, flicking air against Jonathan's stomach. "Mika's not going to scar you. She's a healer."

"I've never met a healer who could do *that* before," Dresden said, gesturing over my shoulder.

Reluctantly, hesitantly, I twisted toward the meadow, hoping it would be too dark . . .

Despite the fading daylight, no one could miss the unnatural snow-white quartz artery spearing from the river-bank through the dusk-drenched field and into the trees.

The sight stole my breath. The band of quartz was so

much wider than I remembered. And longer. Displaced soil and roots mounded to either side, and a ship's worth of flotsam littered the liquid-smooth surface—broken wooden planks and pillars, ripped fabric, torn books, shattered ceramics, and warped metal knobs and railings. Like a bizarre stone tsunami, the shimmering quartz swelled as it flowed away from the river, at first no taller than a step, then curving higher than my head, and higher still, lifting past the tops of the evergreens it had toppled.

The final amber rays of sunset illuminated the tip of the peak and the *Forbidden Splendor* clutched at the precipice. Or what was left of it. Quartz cinched the front of the ship in a vise grip, the sides of the wave rising to clasp the pulverized hull. Of its original fifteen feet of depth, only two remained. Even what we had survived atop, what amounted to little more than a raft, was fractured, held together by ribbons of quartz bonded to the planks.

My hands trembled. I had done that. But it hadn't been me alone. It hadn't been the men I linked with or the gargoyles who boosted us, either, not entirely. It had been the whispers of the baetyl guiding me. Overpowering me. I had thought its powers gone, relinquished to save my sanity and my humanity.

Was I wrong?

My fluttering fingers found Oliver. He watched me with knowing eyes, trust in their depths. I let out a shaky breath and turned to face the men, wondering if it was only my imagination adding wariness to their scrutiny.

"You've probably never met a gargoyle healer before," I said, attempting to deflect their curiosity. But with the *Splendor* practically floating on quartz behind me, I doubted simple words would work.

Across the meadow, Marcus stood with Calidore's squad

mates, a fourth person having emerged from the shadows to join their group. Their heads bent together as they walked the quartz, and they crouched now and again to touch the smooth surface. More than once, their gazes turned toward me.

"How did you do it?" Dresden asked. "I admit to being a bit distracted—"

"Scared out of your mind, you mean," Angus said.

"The same as we all were," Dresden agreed without breaking my gaze. "But I think you and I are almost evenly matched in earth, Mika, and I couldn't follow what you did. How did you know how to . . . ?" He grabbed a handful of soil and lifted it into the air. Dirt rained from his fist. He shook his head and repeated, "How did you do it?"

The men's stares pressed into me, heavy with curiosity. Even Calidore seemed to have forgotten about healing me as he waited to hear my response.

"I don't know," I whispered.

I couldn't explain it, not without speaking of the baetyl, which meant I couldn't speak of it at all. Baetyls were sacred gargoyle hatching grounds, their existence—and their unfathomable powers—a fiercely guarded secret. But without the baetyl's guidance, none of what I did made sense. I didn't even fully remember my own actions, just bits and pieces. If asked, I wouldn't be able to replicate the process. I couldn't even repair the damage I had done to this meadow or retrieve the *Splendor* from its quartz prison.

I saw Dresden's intake of breath, his next question readied. He wouldn't let it go without a more satisfying answer.

"It was desperation magic," I said, speaking first. "I know quartz. I work with it every day. When I'm not healing gargoyles, I'm making quartz figurines and quartz bottles and quartz ornaments. I grabbed hold of what was most familiar to me. It's what made sense at the time. I was so scared, and with everyone linked, I had so much power." The sensation of drawing on the boost of *fourteen* gargoyles ghosted through my mind, the memory as hazy as a dream after waking. Only Oliver and Felix had been present, but within the link, their enhancements had been manifested in each man's magic, multiplying them. Had I truly used their boosts seven times over? Was that even possible, or had it been my imagination?

I shook my head. "It all happened so fast. I did what I thought would keep us alive. Beyond that, I can't remember what magic I used."

Every word I spoke was the truth, and yet it fell far short of a plausible explanation.

"Are you sure Mika did that?" Patrick asked.

I had all but forgotten that the *Happy Hopper*'s pilot was present, and I breathed a sigh of relief when everyone's attention swung to him.

"Are you sure it wasn't Velasquez? I know the man doesn't look like much, but he can sling the elements with passing skill."

Patrick's monumental understatement garnered a few chuckles, and the tension saturating the air dissipated. Calidore tore another splinter from my foot, brushing soothing water after it.

"We're positive," Nicholas said. "If you'd been locked in that link, you would be, too."

Locked?

Calidore shot me a puzzled look, and I shrugged. Terror could play strange tricks on the mind.

"You had me fooled, Mika," Patrick said. "That whole trembly, I've-never-flown bit made me wonder what Velasquez—" He caught himself, but it was easy to guess what he had been about to say: he had wondered what Marcus saw in me.

Clearing his throat, Patrick added a hasty, "I never would have guessed you had this in you." He swept a hand toward the quartz, but no one was paying attention to him anymore.

"This was your first flight?" Dresden asked, his eyes widening comically.

"Ever?" Angus whispered, looking equally as shocked.

"First and last, I'm sure," Patrick said.

"No one would fault you," Jonathan said, placing a commiserative hand on my shoulder.

Marvelous. With one comment, Patrick had transformed me from someone the men viewed with awe into someone pitiable. It was a good thing, I told myself. At least everyone's attention had been diverted from my lack of answers.

My gaze returned to the flow of quartz, and I nibbled my bottom lip queasily. An echo of the baetyl's vast power thrummed at the edges of my awareness, *there* in the twist of quartz where it emerged from the ground, *there* again in the swirl of motion suspended at the apex. The design was flawed, lacking the perfection of the baetyl. But it held hints of it, enough to tease my memory and quicken my pulse.

The song Oliver crooned to me to soothe my fears on the *Hopper* flowed through my mind, breaking apart in my throat when I tried to hum it. I recognized it now as a baetyl's song, the harmony that called to gargoyles.

That called to *me*.

The clarity of the realization stole my breath. If I could peer deep enough inside myself, I knew I would find a thread of the baetyl woven through my subconscious, imprinted on my soul. It was the reason I could sense gargoyles as if I were one of them. It was also the reason we were alive, a blessing bestowed when I thought the baetyl had abandoned me.

"Hey, are you all right?" Jonathan asked, his hand rubbing briskly up and down my back.

I blinked, and twin tears splashed down my cheeks. Startled, I wiped them away with my fingertips.

"I'm fine. Just grateful," I said. I laughed through more tears, shaking my head at Jonathan's questioning look. I couldn't explain it, and I didn't try. Instead, I kissed Oliver's muzzle, and he grinned at me, seeming to understand.

"All done," Calidore announced, setting my foot in the dirt.

"Thank you," I said, sobering as my attention shifted to Felix. Bracing a hand beside my hip, I pushed to my feet. Halfway there, my vision tunneled, and the ground tipped sideways. I collapsed onto my butt with a squeak. Warm hands circled my arms and braced my shoulders, supporting me until my vision cleared and the earth stopped spinning. Marcus halted, having sprinted halfway back to me. I waved a hand to let him know I was all right. His eyes narrowed, sweeping over my face, then my companions. His lips flattened as he took in Nicholas pressed to my side, and something dark swam through his eyes when Jonathan brushed a lock of hair behind my ear. Someone behind Marcus called to him, and with a final glower, he turned away.

"What was that little stunt?" Calidore asked.

"Let's call it attempt one," I said, gathering myself to stand again.

"Oh, you're one of those patients." Calidore planted a hand on my knee and leaned a fraction of his weight on it, immobilizing me. "You need to rest."

"I need to heal Felix."

The small gargoyle's suffering ate at me. He lay perfectly still against Liran, tracking the conversation with his eyes but not lifting his head. He had been through the same terrifying ordeal as the rest of us, nearly falling over the edge of the *Splendor* when we tore free of the aerie and being jostled and bounced around during our harrowing crash, and he had done it all with a broken wing. His pain had to be excruciating.

Brushing aside Calidore's hand, I tensed my thighs and grasped Oliver's wing, trusting him to help me stand and keep me upright. Before I could rock forward, Nicholas dropped a heavy hand on my shoulder.

"I'll bring him to you," he said. He rose with ease and strode around Dresden.

I crossed my arms and tried not to look like I was pouting.

"I would advise against using the elements for a day or two," Calidore said. "You put a lot of strain on your mind with that landing. Like you said, you're not a full spectrum, and my healing can only do so much."

"It was enough."

"Mika, don't be stubborn. You could hurt yourself all over again."

I pulled my gaze from Felix, who had finally lifted his head, his tall ears perking as he listened to our conversation. Meeting Calidore's earnest brown eyes, I let him see my resolution.

"Can you heal Felix?" I asked.

Calidore shook his head.

"I can, and a headache isn't going to stop me."

Calidore huffed, but a small smile curved his lips. "Do you want to link?"

"Thank you, but I have Oliver's boost. It's more than

enough." Turning to Oliver, I said, "I'm going to need seed crystals. Four. No, five. Do you know where my bag is?"

"I do. I'll be right back." Oliver hopped over Jonathan's leg and trundled away from the group before taking flight. Dirt sprayed from his paws, and weeds and dust billowed into the air from the downdraft of his wings, but Dresden swept it aside with a gentle countercurrent.

Firelight glinted off Oliver's carnelian body, turning the stone dragon into an ethereal being of light and shadows. My heart flew with him, phantom wings beating against my back. I breathed through the sensation, savoring it without allowing it to morph into bitterness. I couldn't fly, but I had my own talents, and they were more than enough.

Nicholas lowered Felix to the ground in front of me, and I tucked my feet beneath me, scooting close to inspect him. The steady light of my glowball refracted off nicks and gouges in his obsidian flesh, revealing raw scratches marring the beautiful yellow agate rosettes along his narrow marten belly. Those were fresh, unlike the half inch of stone fluff missing from the tip of his tail and the jagged fracture running through one ear. Even without a broken wing, Felix would have needed healing.

"I'm going to begin," I said to Felix. "If you need me to stop or pause, just say so."

He nodded. Nicholas readied a blade of fire to slice away the rope sling, but I gestured for him to wait. Grabbing the elements through Oliver's boost, I tuned them to Felix's body and eased them into the gargoyle. Pain roared through the link between us, stealing my breath. I hastily cocooned the edges of Felix's broken wing, wrapping numbing elements around the shattered quartz.

Felix's head slumped to the ground, his eyes closing. He took a deep breath, tension easing from his spine.

"Now you can cut the rope," I said. I held my hands beneath Felix's wing, and when the rope fell away, I gently lowered the tip to the ground, layering more numbing elements into the broken segment.

The bundle of energy in my head announced Oliver's return before he landed awkwardly on three feet, his wings fanning fast to catch his balance. Someone built a protective dome around us, blocking the dust and preventing the fire from being blown out. Then Oliver lumbered to my side and spilled seed crystals into my lap.

"Thank you." I gave him a quick smile, then selected a seed. Dividing my attention between the numbing spell on Felix's wing and a new weave of elements, I tuned the pure quartz to match the living onyx of Felix's body. The quartz crystal stretched in my grip, reshaping to match the gargoyle's wound. When I leaned forward to place the seed, Dresden bent with me, his head so close his hair tickled the side of my face. I hesitated. Before I could say anything, Oliver snaked his muzzle in front of Dresden and puffed out a reproachful breath. Startled, Dresden jerked back, giving me room.

Rolling my lips inward to hide my smile, I delicately set the seed against Felix's broken wing. Building connections between the gargoyle's living tissue and the new quartz consumed my attention, and I forgot about Dresden hovering over my shoulder or the weight of the other men's curious stares. At some point Patrick, or perhaps Calidore, asked how the men had gotten caught in the aerie. Snippets of the men's story filtered through my concentration, enough to piece together a tale of bad timing and worse luck.

They had fallen asleep above a peaceful lake and woke when the *Splendor* capsized. Disoriented and battered, they had been trapped in their flooding cabins, unable to power through the influx of water. Liran and Angus had suffered the worst of it, half crushed when an interior wall collapsed on them. None of them even knew they were inside an aerie until Nicholas attempted to swim to the surface for help. With the men trapped, it fell to Felix to fly for assistance. But once outside the aerie, Felix realized his friends were too weak to survive the awanyus' magic without his boost, and he plunged back into the aerie.

The gargoyle had been injured during reentry. With the interior of the *Splendor* in shambles, floating furniture and other belongings clogging the cramped cabins, the deck had been the safest place for Felix.

"We would have drowned without Felix," Nicholas said. "Wielding magic in there was like pulling the elements through wool. You felt it, Mika. We couldn't get enough power behind our spells to free Liran or Angus. Eventually we stopped trying and focused on maintaining the breathing filters and arresting Liran's bleeding. The awanyus couldn't fly forever. Our only option was to wait them out." His voice grew softer at the last statement, and the men exchanged knowing glances.

None of them had expected to last until the awanyus landed for the night.

"How did you know we were in the aerie?" Angus asked.

"Your gargoyle, of course," Patrick said. "Oliver sensed him and let us know."

I kept my head tucked over Felix's wing, happy to leave the explanation at that. A third seed crystal finally closed the break in his wing, and I layered connecting elements between the raw quartz and Felix's obsidian flesh. Mindful of my limits and the headache building behind my eyes, I took a break before using the last of the seed crystals to patch his cuts and scratches. The older injuries troubled me the most; I hated knowing Felix had suffered these aches for years without seeking out—or even knowing he *could* seek out—healing.

"I think we're all wondering how five such, ah, pretty men came to travel together," Patrick said. "Unless, of course, that's a private matter between you. A, uh, *forbidden* thing of love that I shouldn't speak of and all that."

For a long second, silence reigned. Then Angus guffawed and Jonathan chuckled.

"My *cousins* and I are performers," Angus said.

"Actors?" Patrick didn't appear convinced.

"We perform for specific audiences. Typically female," Nicholas said. "Feats of strength. Feats of skill."

"Feats of beauty," Jonathan said. He shifted with calculated precision, flexing his abdomen so his muscles appeared to roll.

"Burlesque actors? But for women?" Patrick's question came out high with shock.

"It's still called burlesque, no matter who the audience is," Nicholas said.

"Though we prefer 'all-male traveling troupe,'" Angus said.

"We tailor our act to the audience. At fairs, we're not so…"

"Sensual?" Calidore offered.

"But we give the ladies what they want when the shows are more adult oriented."

I did *not* glance up to see whatever gyrations Jonathan accompanied to his words. Nevertheless, a blush crept up my neck. I had heard of troupes like theirs, and seeing them, I could picture it all too well. It also explained why the men looked like they belonged in the FPD despite rather ordinary magical skills.

"You've got to show me how you did that," Patrick said, standing. He wiggled his torso experimentally, the stripes on his shirt dancing dizzyingly. "If I had moves like that, I might be able to, ahem, 'fly a ship' on every continent, if you catch my drift."

I rolled my eyes.

"How do you fit in, Felix?" I asked.

"They are my home," the gargoyle said simply, and I was gratified to hear no pain in his voice.

"Felix spent many years with my distant aunt," Nicholas said. "She was a full spectrum with a full-spectrum husband. Sadly, they had no children. When she passed, I asked Felix if he would like to live with us."

"There's always plenty of magic around," Felix said.

My protective instincts relaxed. Gargoyles tended to live with full-spectrum families or in populous locations because they needed the influx of elements to stay healthy. The men might not be powerful enough to support a gargoyle on their own, but their lifestyle ensured Felix maintained a well-balanced diet.

"You don't mind the travel?" I asked.

"I never had to leave the *Splendor* if I didn't want to, but seeing some of the world has made me curious about seeing more."

"I can understand that," Oliver said.

Felix smiled. Above his head, Dresden and Nicholas shared surprised glances, as if they hadn't considered a gargoyle might not enjoy their vagabond lifestyle.

"That's the last of it," I announced, sighing softly when I released the elements and my headache eased to a dull thump in tempo with my pulse. I straightened, spine popping, and yawned.

Felix flexed his wing, cautiously at first, then more quickly. The clear quartz patch glinted in the firelight, bright against his ebony body. He stretched, then pranced in place, his movements increasingly animated.

"I haven't felt this wonderful in forever," he exclaimed.

"Any time you need healing, you can find me in Terra Haven. Ask any gargoyle in the city. They all know where I live."

"Thank you." Felix rubbed his muzzle into my hand.

"You're astounding, Mika," Dresden said. "I watched every step, and I still have no idea how you did that. Again. We owe you for our lives, and I'm not sure how to repay that debt, but please let me pay you for healing Felix."

I shook my head. Charging these men after their ship and belongings had been destroyed didn't feel right. "It was my pleasure."

"We have plenty of money, this aside." Dresden waved a hand toward the pulverized *Splendor*. "And I can't think of a more worthy way to spend it than on making our friend feel so good."

Felix preened for Calidore and Angus, showing off his glossy toes and scratch-free stomach, his tongue lolling happily from his mouth. I couldn't help but smile.

When my gaze returned to Dresden, a hint of distress marred his happiness. He obviously cared greatly for Felix. I wondered how long the gargoyle hadn't been at his best, and if Dresden was only just now understanding the silent suffering Felix had endured.

"I owe you so much," Dresden said, his voice soft, almost pleading.

Realizing my refusal prevented Dresden from showing

his gratitude—and perhaps from assuaging some of his guilt—I quoted my usual rate, then added, "And you have to promise you'll tell every gargoyle you meet about me. I want them to know they can come to me if they need help."

"Deal," Dresden said and shook my hand, then pulled me into a seated hug and whispered in my ear, "But I'm going to tip you double."

"You don't need—"

"And next time we're in Terra Haven, we're taking you out to dinner."

I pictured all five of these handsome men showing up on the doorstep of Ms. Zuberrie's Victorian house. My landlady would be speechless—and secretly thrilled to tell all her friends about it later.

"I look forward to it," I said.

A throat cleared, and I turned to find Marcus standing at the edge of the firelight, watching me with unreadable eyes. I dropped my hand from Dresden's arm. Marcus's eyes tracked the movement before returning to mine. He had acquired a long-sleeve black shirt, and the soft cotton molded to his chest and biceps. It had to be his—no one else's clothing would have fit him so well—and it made the blue of his eyes that much brighter in contrast. I longed to drag my fingers through his mussed hair and trace my nails along the stubble darkening his jaw. I needed tactile reassurance he was safe and whole.

"Finally someone has the decency to cover their nipples," Patrick said. "You're all making Calidore self-conscious."

I blinked, a blush springing to my cheeks when I realized I had forgotten the other men existed. Dropping my gaze, I spotted our bags at Marcus's feet, my boots lined up beside them. When had he retrieved those?

"We're done here for tonight," a stocky woman in an FPD uniform said, striding into the light. Her collar bore a fire symbol, making her the same rank as Marcus, though her demeanor indicated she was the captain of her squad. "How long until this one is ready for travel?" She pointed to Liran, still unconscious on the air stretcher.

"He's ready now," Calidore said. He stood and brushed dirt from his pants. "I've healed all but his surface bruises, but it took a lot out of him. I think he'll sleep all the way to Sumac Springs."

"Good. We'll return tomorrow with Toussaint and Helgenberger and see if we can't make something of this mess." Her gaze fell from the quartz peak to land on me. I squirmed, waiting for questions I couldn't answer, but all she said was, "A gargoyle guardian?"

"Yes, ma'am."

"Huh. All right. We've got room in the air carts for everyone if we squeeze real close. Velasquez, we can have you on a train back to Terra Haven by tomorrow afternoon."

"Thank you," Marcus said.

I clicked my mouth shut. Air carts meant low-to-the-ground air travel—the natural kind of travel. And a train! Safely connected to metal rails locked to the ground. Relief sang through my veins. I could be home in a day or two, sleeping in my own bed, air travel once more relegated to my nightmares.

Felix launched into the air, soaring out over the meadow. I lost sight of him against the deepening gloom, but I tracked his progress by the bundle of energy in my head. It glowed brighter than before but was still weaker than Oliver's. Another day or two without wounds sapping his strength, and Felix would be back to full health.

Oliver and I were the only two people who didn't jump

when Felix coasted between Calidore and Marcus. The gargoyle landed lightly, his throaty chuckle half garbled as he galloped around the rim of the fire and threw himself at Dresden. With practiced ease, Dresden caught the stone marten in a clutch of air and cradled him to his chest.

I grinned down at the squirming gargoyle, suffused with joy at the sight of his pain-free wriggles. I had made that possible.

Nicholas and Jonathan helped me to my feet, fussing over me with gentle spells that swept dirt from my hair and clothes while I remembered how to stand on my own. Both insisted on a hug, pulling me tight to their bare chests and thanking me again for saving their lives. Then Dresden tugged me into an embrace around Felix, and Angus was ready with a hug of his own when Dresden released me. In between each breath-stealing squeeze, I puzzled over Marcus's hardening expression. His eyes grew flinty. His jaw muscle began to tick. One hand fisted, then he crossed his arms.

Jonathan said something, brushing my arm to get my attention. Marcus's eyes tracked the motion, and I froze, rooted in place by utter astonishment as I finally interpreted the emotions playing across Marcus's face.

My boyfriend, the confident warrior who had single-handedly saved us with the kind of skill and strength that inspired legends—this incredible man was *jealous*.

It boggled my mind. Because jealousy implied an insecurity, a fear of losing me.

My stomach flipped when Marcus's gaze finally collided with mine. Fire smoldered in those blue depths, but it was the vulnerability beneath the heat that speared straight to my heart. Marcus was afraid of something. It might seem insignificant compared to all that scared me, especially since I knew his fear was unfounded. But it was proof Marcus had flaws, like me.

A knot in my gut unraveled, stretching hope toward the future. Our future. One where we helped each other overcome our fears—together.

Smiling, I rested a hand on Oliver's forehead, and without taking my eyes off Marcus, asked, "Patrick, can the *Happy Hopper* fly?"

Marcus frowned.

"Don't worry, Mika," Patrick said. "I'll be fine. Liz and the others helped repair my skipper while you were getting your beauty sleep. As soon as you're off—"

"Do you still have room for three more?" I interrupted.

Marcus jolted a step toward me, then kept coming, stopping close enough to grip my biceps. His eyes searched mine.

"Are you sure?" he asked.

The thought of climbing back aboard the *Hopper* sent a tremble through my knees. Picturing the land receding below us left me dizzy. But I had done it once before, and I'd survived. I had *crashed* and survived.

If I had given in to my phobia of heights back in Terra Haven, Felix would be dead. So would his friends. But Marcus and Oliver had helped me be braver than my terror. And that was all I needed to be: just a little bit braver. I didn't have to be a paragon of courage. So long as I didn't allow fear to dictate my actions, I would be worthy of being a gargoyle guardian.

"I'm sure," I said, tipping my chin high so Marcus could read the certainty in my eyes. "With you at my side—both of you," I added, including Oliver, "I can do this."

Pride shone in Marcus's eyes, erasing the last traces of

doubt from his expression. "There's nowhere I'd rather be," he whispered before his lips brushed mine.

"We're going to have to fly extra fast to make up for lost time," Patrick said.

I took Marcus's hand, reassured by his firm grip against my damp palm. "Good. Because we need to make it to the everlasting tree before it blooms."

I had more gargoyles to save.

SPECIAL BONUS

Receive the ebook *Lured* for free!

Join Rebecca's VIP List and receive *Lured*, a short tale featuring fan-favorite characters from the Gargoyle Guardian Chronicles.

https://www.rebeccachastain.com/newsletter/

DON'T MISS KYLIE & QUINN'S FIRST ADVENTURE!

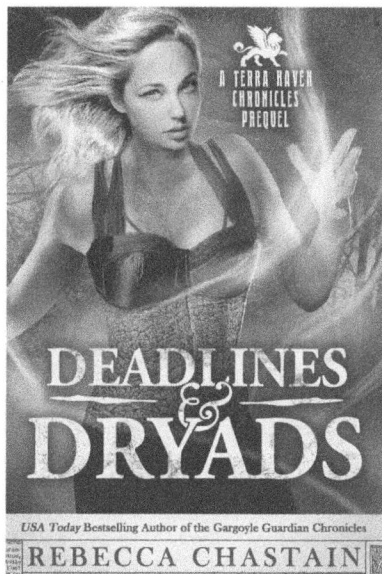

PRAISE FOR *DEADLINES & DRYADS*

"a fabulous, lighthearted read"
–*Tome Tender* ★★★★★

"fun and fast paced"
–*Feeling Fictional*

RebeccaChastain.com

EXCERPT: DEADLINES & DRYADS

I drummed my fingers on my open notebook, resisting the urge to bounce in my seat. Tension crackled in the charged air of the writers' bullpen, where every single *Terra Haven Chronicle* reporter had gathered this morning at the behest of the editor in chief. She'd given no reason for the meeting, and speculations buzzed through the curiosity-saturated atmosphere.

"Does this happen often?" I asked the junior journalist next to me, who had been at the paper a few months longer than me. I had to raise my voice to be heard above the energized hubbub.

"No. Whatever's going on, it's big."

The editor's door cracked open, and all conversations in the room died off. Everyone leaned forward when Raquel Jervier, the newspaper's gryphon scout, sauntered out. She swept her gaze over our rapt faces and grinned, her white teeth bright against her dark face. Unperturbed by everyone's intense scrutiny, she took a seat at an empty desk, leaning the chair back on two legs to prop her heavy boots on the desk's corner. The writer nearest her started to whisper a question but immediately quieted when Dahlia Bearpaw, the editor in chief, strode into the bullpen, coffee cup in hand. With spiky gray hair and a wiry, regal bearing, Dahlia looked as much a gryphon rider as Raquel—and had been in her youth. Now she ran the paper with the same firm hand.

"I think I might have a riot in here if I don't get right to the point," Dahlia said, taking in our eager expressions. "So, here's the deal: The western everlasting tree is starting to bud."

A collective exclamation of excitement exploded across the room, but I remained frozen in place, my thoughts pinging so fast that I temporarily forgot how to move. Forty years ago, one of the immortal trees in Asia had bloomed. It had been the first everlasting tree to show signs of fertility in centuries, and people had flocked to it. Standing beneath its blooming branches, they had asked their myriad questions. In response, the tree had unleashed a flurry of seeds, one per person, no two seeds alike. Just as legend had foretold, the seeds had served as maps of sorts, guiding each person to their answers—if they put in the time and due diligence. It hadn't mattered the nature of their inquiries—personal or professional, selfish or altruistic; the tree had answered them all.

Everlasting trees were as rare as their bloomings; fewer than two existed per continent, and each released its seeds once every century, if not once every half millennium. I never thought an everlasting tree would bloom in my lifetime, especially not the tree nearest Terra Haven.

"Calm down. I know it's exciting, but I haven't finished my announcement," Dahlia shouted above the uproar. "The

Chronicle is going to send two journalists." Silence dropped over the room as every writer leaned in, waiting to hear who she would select. "The lead journalist on the story will be Audrey Cintrón, but I have yet to pick who will accompany her."

A sea of envious gazes swept to Audrey, who exchanged a solemn nod with the editor. A veteran journalist with decades of experience at the *Chronicle*, Audrey had earned her right to attend this monumental event. Her elegant, precise prose made her the perfect choice, and I strove to rein in my jealousy. From my table at the back of the room, cramped elbow to elbow with the other first-year journalists, I studied the remaining senior writers with a bitter eye. This was a story of a lifetime, and it had come years too early for me.

I mentally tabulated my savings, my connections, and my current standing at the paper. I didn't have the finances to reach the everlasting tree on my own, and I didn't know anybody with the resources to get me there, either. Even if I did, I couldn't afford to take the weeks off work the trip would necessitate, not if I expected to have my job waiting for me when I got home. A knot of resentment settled in my gut, and I leaned back in my chair, defeated.

"Before you all bombard me with your qualifications— which I already know, or you wouldn't be here," Dahlia continued, "let me deliver the second part of this announcement. The position for the second journalist will be determined by whoever brings me the best story in the next forty-eight hours."

I shot from my chair so fast it tumbled over backward. I had a chance!

The room around me had erupted in similar reactions,

though several senior writers looked less than pleased. I couldn't muster any sympathy for them. I had written a few good articles for the paper, which was why I had a seat in this room, but I was far from one of the editors' go-to writers when it came to handing out assignments. If I could win this competition, not only would it prove to Dahlia that I had what it took to cover the everlasting tree, but it would also cement my career at the *Chronicle*.

Dahlia's astute gaze cataloged everyone's reactions, including mine as I sheepishly straightened my chair. When she called for silence again, everyone was quick to comply.

"You may have noticed Hernando isn't here today. I sent him out before dawn to cover an invasion of poisonous serpents spotted in Lincoln River, upstream of the city. You'll need to top that story to have a shot at winning."

A collective groan spiraled around the room. Lincoln River flowed straight through Terra Haven and served as the main source of drinking water for a greater portion of the city. The deadly serpents would be a huge story for the *Chronicle*, and one not easily topped.

My hand shot into the air, and I waved it around to get the editor's attention, but she was already pivoting in my direction.

"Unsurprisingly, the first question comes from junior journalist Kylie Grayson," Dahlia said, her tone wry.

"She's always got the most questions because she doesn't have a clue what she's doing," Nathan said, pitching his voice to carry across the room from his corner desk in the senior writers' section.

I ignored him. I wouldn't let him shame my curiosity. "When will the chosen journalists leave?" I asked.

"As soon as I've made my selection," Dahlia said. "Even

traveling gryphonback, the trip will take you several days, and we can't predict when the everlasting tree will release its seeds. I want reporters on the ground posthaste. This is a once-in-a-generation story that deserves more than a few articles; I want to run a special edition, perhaps a series of special editions."

I hadn't thought the room could get any more tense, but at the potent words *special edition*, every single writer went on point. A special edition would mean dozens of articles. Split between only two journalists, we'd each get entire spreads to fill. Contemplating all that column space left me light-headed with yearning.

"One last thing," Dahlia said. "If you've got the vacation time and you'd rather attend the blooming at your own expense, I'll accept the first five vacation requests."

Half the room surged toward the editor, and in the chaos, I slipped out the back. I didn't have the vacation time to use even if I did have the money to get halfway across the country in a few days.

I passed through the exit into the sunlight and paused, realizing I didn't know where to go. I had a few rumor scouts in the field, and I had a few leads I could follow up on, but would any of them evolve into a story spectacular enough to win me this competition?

I pulled my journal out of my bag and opened it to peruse my notes, moving to the edge of the sidewalk to get out of the way of foot traffic. The city had woken up while I'd been inside, and the downtown streets bustled with people headed to their jobs. A horse-drawn wagon trundled past, the driver fighting the reins as the team shied at the sight of the enormous gryphon perched atop the *Chronicle*'s two-story roof. I tilted my head back and acknowledged the tiny shiver of fear that darted down my spine when the gryphon cocked her massive eagle head and pinned me with a golden eye. Rationally, I knew she was Raquel's tame companion and would never eat a human, but my instincts still kicked in, telling me to run. Suppressing them, I scanned the rest of the roofline for Quinn's bright citrine face, but when I didn't spot the gargoyle, I turned back to my notebook.

The door burst open beside me, and Nathan stepped out, sweeping his dark hair off his forehead in a practiced motion. Lanky, with a perpetual black, bristly beard and thick-framed glasses, he looked like a caricature of a hard-working investigative reporter—a style he'd obviously culti-vated. He spotted me and grinned, spinning on a toe to confront me.

"Tell me that was for show," he said. "You don't *actually* believe you can snag a story that's more impressive than anything a senior writer can get, do you?"

"You heard Dahlia. We all have a shot."

"Come on, Kylie. You've been here less than six months. You don't have a chance."

"I've had two front-page stories already," I said, knowing I shouldn't let him goad me but unable to help myself. "How many front-page stories have you had in that time?"

Nathan's thin lips tightened and he shoved his hands into his pockets. Score one for me.

"You got lucky. Twice," he said. "But this time you can't just wait around for an article to fall into your lap. Or do you plan to pump your gargoyle friend for another story?"

I pushed my hair out of my face and gave him my best glare. I hated that he was partially right; I had been lucky in landing two major stories before anybody else knew they were happening, thanks to my best friend, Mika. In the last couple months, she had rescued several gargoyles and had become the city's one and only gargoyle healer. The very first story that had gotten me noticed by Dahlia had been the tale of Mika's daring rescue of the gargoyles. A small part of me wished I were bringing that story to the editor now, because it would have guaranteed me a victory in this competition. Now I needed to present Dahlia with something even more impressive, and every lead in my notebook fell well short.

Not that I would admit as much to Nathan.

"Don't worry about me," I said, injecting false sweetness into my voice. "I already have another amazing story lined up."

"You do? Just like that?"

"I do." I managed to infuse confidence I didn't feel into those two words.

Tilting my journal so Nathan couldn't see its contents, I scanned my notes again. Maybe the thefts at the fish market would develop into something bigger than petty crime. If not, I might be able to spin the story into a larger commentary addressing the socioeconomic disparities . . . Ugh. No. Maybe I *would* have to hunt down Mika and see if she had encountered any new gargoyles in trouble. Of course, Dahlia might not be impressed with a third story in a row about gargoyles.

"You're riding high on your past successes, but don't let your beginner's luck fool you," Nathan cautioned, his patronizing tone setting my teeth on edge. "Do yourself a favor and don't burn yourself out trying to compete with experienced journalists. Put in the time, put in the legwork, and you'll eventually pull in some big stories on your own."

This wasn't the first time Nathan had given me his "sage advice," which basically amounted to *take it slow* and *don't upstage senior writers*. I had no intention of listening to him. "I'm not sure why you're concerned about what I'm going to write if you're so certain your story will be superior."

"Oh, I'm not worried. It's just I see promise in you, and I don't want you to get your spirit crushed before you even start your career."

Two front-page stories! I wanted to shout. My career had already started, and it'd begun with a bang.

"I'm flattered you noticed my journalistic skills. Excuse me, Nathan, I've got to run." I snapped my journal shut and stalked off before he could say anything else—or before I said something I'd regret.

I hadn't made it halfway down the block when I spotted my rumor scout barreling down on me. The snarl of elemental energy whipped through the air, tight bands of air and fire woven through thinner strands of earth, water, and wood, all of it holding precious information. I glanced back over my shoulder and picked up my pace. Nathan tracked my retreat, and his eyes narrowed when he caught sight of my elemental creation. Damn it.

Half jogging, I met the rumor scout at the end of the block. Shaped from my magic, it honed in on me with a precision that had taken years to perfect. I shoved my hair out of the way as the bundle of magic coiled over my right ear, forming a soundproof seal against my scalp. Immediately, a stranger's voice spoke into my ear, the words having been collected and recorded by the scout.

"... dryad chased me. I've never seen anything like it. I've taken Wicker Road hundreds of times, and I've seen my share of dryads, but not like this." The man's deep voice held the accent of a Southern merchant, and he sounded out of breath. He didn't pause to give whoever he was talking to a chance to speak, either. "The dryads looked . . . they looked, well . . . predatory."

Predatory? Dryads were peaceful creatures. They lived in harmony with the trees to which their lives were bonded, and their personalities were the equivalent of an oak given mobility. They nurtured the forest and they lived quiet, hidden lives. I couldn't even picture what a predatory dryad would look like; it was like trying to picture a hostile tree—one that had apparently chased this man.

My journalistic instincts perked up.

I had been hearing rumors about increased restlessness in the local Emerald Crown Grove dryads since the tail end of winter, which was why I'd tailored a rumor scout to seek out and record any conversations in which the word *dryad* was mentioned. I'd also read up on dryads at the city library, learning that their abnormal agitation could be due to an impending violent storm or a possible encroachment of a new road or predator into their grove. I'd held off pitching the story to Dahlia because I had my own, third theory that involved the timing of the dryads' restlessness, but I'd been waiting for it to pan out.

I hadn't even considered that the dryad story might be worthy of today's challenge, but this new development held promise. Maybe I wouldn't need to go to the fish market after all.

"Don't do it," the anxious voice continued. "You don't want to chance—"

Claws of air magic ripped the rumor scout from my ear, tearing out a hunk of my hair.

"Ow!"

I spun around. Nathan clutched my rumor scout in a

thick lasso of air and held it suspended in front of him, studying it with avid curiosity.

Double damn.

—————

Keep reading *Deadlines & Dryads*. Pick up your copy today!

ACKNOWLEDGMENTS

Thank you for reading Mika and Oliver's latest adventure! This book would not exist without your support of the original trilogy. I'm especially grateful for every person who wrote me asking for more Mika books! You kept me inspired to return to this world and these characters.

I am incredibly fortunate to have a superb team at my back, including my beta readers Pam Morarre, Sarah Gibson, Rebecca Moore, Seana Waldon, Jillian Cori Lippert, Scott Ferguson, and Renea Kania. Each of these wonderful people provided unique insights that improved the book in little and large ways. Many thanks also go to my talented copyeditor, Crystal Watanabe, and proofreader, Cheryl Murphy Lowrance, for giving this book a final polish and making me look good.

For emotional support, technical support, what's-that-word-I'm-thinking-of support, please-feed-the-cats-so-they-stop-yelling-at-me support, and so much more, Cody, you have my endless gratitude. You're the best writer's spouse a woman could dream (or write) up.

Do you ever wonder where I get the ideas for my novels? Well . . . this time we have my mom to thank. After a year of the pandemic, all I wanted was a fun and light project to recharge my creative energy. I knew I needed to launch Mika toward the everlasting tree, but I wasn't sure what would happen on her journey. While in the brainstorming phase, I hinted at a few ideas in an email to my mom, and she wrote this back:

Hmm, in an airship flying to the everlasting tree. She is blown off course . . . into whatever her question starts with trials and quests and gargoyles and naked men (just kidding), and ?

But that *just kidding* sparked an idea. I responded:

Naked men? I kind of like that idea for Mika's story. It would make her love interest, Marcus, jealous. Or not, depending on the state of the naked men. Are they running across an old-man nude colony, or is it a bunch of twentysomethings competing in a ceremony that involves a lot of nudity except for a loincloth?

Thankfully, I didn't go with my first idea. (No one needs to spend their time envisioning nude old men!) The second idea obviously didn't pan out, either, but naked men stuck around through the brainstorming.

So thank you, Teri! This book would have been lacking a lot of fun visuals if not for you!

ABOUT THE AUTHOR

REBECCA CHASTAIN is a feminist, animal advocate, and nature devotee. She believes empathy is a hero's trait and love is a motive, an inside job, and a transformative energy that shapes each person's world. She is the *USA Today* best-selling author of the Gargoyle Guardian Chronicles series, the Terra Haven Chronicles series that begins with *Deadlines & Dryads* and the Madison Fox urban fantasy series.

If given the opportunity, Rebecca will befriend your cat.

Visit RebeccaChastain.com
for free stories, bonus materials, updates, and so much
more!

Join Rebecca online
Facebook: facebook.com/rebeccachastainnovels
Twitter: @Author_Rebecca
Instagram: @chastain.rebecca

FROM *USA TODAY*
BESTSELLING AUTHOR

REBECCA CHASTAIN

**Madison's new job would be perfect,
if not for all the creatures trying to
eat her soul...**

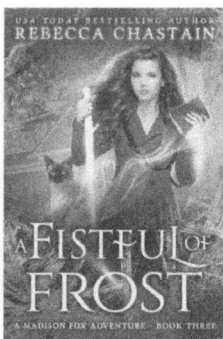

PRAISE FOR THE MADISON FOX NOVELS

"a masterfully plotted urban fantasy... I highly
recommend it to readers of all ilk, urban fantasy
aficionados, or not."
–Open Book Society

"a great mixture of action, danger, fantasy,
and humor"
–Books That Hook

RebeccaChastain.com

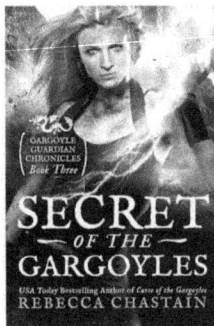

Don't miss a one-of-a-kind hilarious adventure
from *USA Today* bestselling author

Rebecca Chastain

TINY GLITCHES

Dealing with her electricity-killing curse
makes living in modern-day Los Angeles
complicated for Eva—and that was before
she was blackmailed into hiding a stolen
baby elephant and on the run with Hudson,
a sexy electrical engineer she just met.

"I laughed out loud too many times to count."
–Pure Textuality

RebeccaChastain.com

www.ingramcontent.com/pod-product-compliance
Ingram Content Group UK Ltd.
Pitfield, Milton Keynes, MK11 3LW, UK
UKHW011447041125
8755UKWH00013B/37

9 781734 493979